ARIZONA SKYLINE

A year ago, Ron Garroway was in the right place at the wrong time: searching for land to start a ranch near the fledgling town of Prescott, Arizona, he fell in with two men who robbed a bank with a confederate. Although on a scouting expedition at the time, Ron was named as the third man just before the two convicts were hanged. Tired of running, he knows he must return to Prescott to clear his name. On the stage journey he meets the beautiful Christine Mayberry, travelling from Ohio to discover why her prospector father disappeared from the town without a trace nine years ago. Ron finds himself entangled in the mystery — but he never anticipated getting kidnapped as soon as he arrives by a couple of hardcases after the money they're convinced he's stashed away from the bank heist . . .

ARIZONA SKYLINE

ALLAN VAUGHAN ELSTON

SAGEBRUSH
Large Print Westerns

First published in Great Britain by Hale
First published in the United States by Berkley Medallion

First Isis Edition
published 2020
by arrangement with
Golden West Literary Agency

A catalogue record for this book is available
from the British Library.

ISBN 978–1–78541–700–9 (pb)

Published by
Ulverscroft Limited
Anstey, Leicestershire

Set by Words & Graphics Ltd.
Anstey, Leicestershire
Printed and bound in Great Britain by
T. J. International Ltd., Padstow, Cornwall

This book is printed on acid-free paper

To the old Daily and Weekly Miner of Prescott —
a sleeping history in the archives of Arizona
— from whose files for the years 1873 to 1882
comes most of the background for this book.

CHAPTER
ONE

The mixed train — one passenger coach, two boxcars, and four flats loaded with bridge irons — rattled to a stop at End-of-Track.

A brakeman shouted: "Everybody out! This is Canyon Diablo, as far as we go. The stage for Prescott's waitin' at the other end of the bridge."

Ron Garroway picked up his bag and stood in the aisle, allowing others to go ahead of him. His muscles were stiff from a day and a night of chair-car travel. Some of the others had ridden a Pullman Palace sleeper as far as Albuquerque, there changing to this half-passenger, half-construction train. Some, like himself, were outsiders bound for Prescott, capital of Arizona Territory. Others lived at Prescott and were on their way home after a brief trip east. All were sleepy-eyed and disheveled after the twelve-hour night run from Albuquerque.

They filed down the coach aisle toward an exit, lugging baggage. The slim, dark girl directly ahead of Ron had two bags. "Let me handle one of them for you," he offered.

"Thank you." She turned with a grateful smile and let him take the bulging Gladstone she was struggling with. "Do you know how far it is to Prescott?"

"A hundred and sixty-five miles, I'm told. Thirty-three hours by stage. This your first trip there?"

"Yes. And yours?"

He wished she hadn't asked it, because it forced him to lie. He was glad she wasn't looking at him when he murmured an affirmative. She was moving forward again, the back of her blue-bonneted head toward him. It was a small, bird-winged bonnet matching the ankle-length, fur-trimmed coat she was wearing. Sitting behind her all night in the dimly lighted coach, he'd become aware that she was uncommonly pretty and probably not over twenty-three. Now it occurred to him bleakly that whatever acquaintance he made with her must be cut short when they got to Prescott.

Directly behind him were two young mining engineers, Haskins and Rudd. He'd talked to them at the Fort Wingate stop and knew they were heading for Prescott because of the mineral boom there.

"Thirty-three hours!" one of them exclaimed. "That only figures five miles an hour!"

A tall, rawboned cowboy in the line heard and answered. He was on his way home from Kansas City after delivering a shipment of Arizona cattle to the market there. "That's right. We change teams eleven times. Won't be that way very long, though. Every time they lay another fifty mile of track, the stage ride gets that much shorter."

The girl was now on the open vestibule, and a brakeman handed her down. Ron followed. When she offered to take her bag from him, he shook his head. "I'll put it on the stage for you. Wonder where it is."

2

Again the tall, wind-weathered cowboy supplied information. "Other side of the hole, folks; reckon they'll have to buckboard us over there."

By "hole" he meant a canyon of awesome depth which cut through the land here, and against which the track-laying had been forced to stop. A half-finished bridge spanned the canyon, to which a crew of workmen was approaching from a huge construction camp on the other side. The chill of early morning and high altitude made the girl turn up the collar of her coat. It was a May morning in the year 1882; and the Atlantic & Pacific Railroad, building westward toward California, could lay its rails no farther until the bridge was completed.

A man in corduroys clapped his hands and announced himself as agent of the Gilmer, Salisbury & Company stage line. "Listen, all you Prescott passengers. You'll get breakfast in a tent dining room on the other side. These two wagons'll ferry you over there. You'll just have time to eat before we start rollin'."

The "wagons" were two-seated buckboards, each with a wind-tattered canvas top. Ron followed the girl to the nearest one, helped her aboard, and took a seat by her. The cowboy and the two young metallurgists got on with them. Other Prescott-bound passengers boarded the second vehicle. Ron's driver cracked his whip, and they began a tortuous descent which twisted down a precipitous wall of Canyon Diablo. The trail switchbacked first to the south, then to the north, then south again. The second buckboard followed.

3

The leading driver turned his head, grinning. "Hang on tight, lady. If you'd come a few months later, you wouldn't need to do this. Bridge'll be done by then. It'll be five hun'erd and forty feet long and nigh three hundred feet high — and 'il cost close to a million dollars. Once it's done they'll lay two miles of track a day on west. Easy there." He applied his brakes as they twisted around another switchback turn.

Finally they reached the gorge's rock bottom and started up a similar trail on the other side. Haskins, in the front seat, turned his head and spoke to Ron. "Got the time, Andrews? My watch stopped."

Arnold Andrews was the name on his ticket and the one under which he'd been living for the past year. Not till he reached the courthouse in Prescott would he identify himself as Ronald Garroway.

"Straight-up seven," he said. Steel-rimmed glasses and a short mustache minimized the risk of his being recognized before the end of his journey. He had a ranching background, but now in his gray topcoat and creased fedora he might be taken for a traveling salesman on his way to sell shoes or hardware to the merchants of Arizona.

After a series of ascending switchbacks they came out on the west rim. Here there was a small tent city housing the bridge-construction crews and a grading outfit. There were two tent saloons, a restaurant, and a tent store. Beyond to the northeast loomed pine-clad mountains with snowy caps. A four-horse Concord coach was drawn up in front of the restaurant tent, and

4

the buckboards stopped there. The entire area was swarming with men and mule teams.

The Gilmer, Salisbury agent herded his passengers in to breakfast. "We'll see that your baggage is loaded," he promised. "While you eat, the driver will pick up your tickets."

Each of them had a ticket which covered both railroad and stagecoach travel. One could, if he wished, buy a through ticket all the way from Chicago to Prescott.

The table was pine boards laid across sawhorses. Food was bacon, fried potatoes, and coffee. While they were eating, the stage driver came in and took their tickets. He was friendly, talkative, bearded, and gunslung. The first ticket he took was the tall cowboy's. "Glad to see you back, Steve," he greeted. "Hope you got a good price for them steers. Folks, seein' as you'll be ridin' together all day today, all night, and most of tomorrow, you might as well know each other. This here's Steve Mulgrave, foreman for the Emily Wardell cattle layout down around Skull Valley."

Steve Mulgrave grinned back at him. "And plenty glad to get home, Jake."

As Jake collected each ticket, he repeated the name on it so that all could hear. "Miss Christine Mayberry. You've come a long way, lady. Cleveland, Ohio. It's a rough road ahead, and I'll try not to bump you too much." He punched her ticket and took Ron's. "Arnold Andrews," he said. "Eat hearty, Mr. Andrews. It's the last grub you'll get till we make Flagstaff."

5

Flagstaff was a new name to Ron. He was sure it hadn't existed when he left this range a year ago.

The driver took tickets from Haskins and Rudd with no comment except to announce their names. The next man, wearing a brown derby, was Dan McCurdy, who operated a popular saloon on the Prescott plaza. "Welcome home, Dan. Didja get them fancy bar fixtures you went to Chicago after?" Jake picked up the next ticket, which belonged to a stranger named Conway. Conway had the look and dress of a prosperous cattleman.

The next man was Wan Sung, a well-known dignitary of Prescott's Chinatown. "Runs a restaurant, laundry, and joss house on Granite Street, folks; he'll take you on at fan-tan or poker, day or night, if you like."

The last ticket he punched belonged to a lawyer named Frank Maxwell. "Frank," Jake announced, "is attorney for the Skyline mine, richest payin' property in Yavapai County. Got its own smelter, the Skyline has. It shipped lots of bullion since you left, Frank. Any of you folks get in sheriff trouble, you better look Frank up."

Maxwell, dark, clean-shaven and fortyish, waved a hand at the table. "Thanks for the free advertising, Jake." He was easily the best dressed and most personable man in the tent.

"We got two more passengers," Jake announced, "who didn't come in on the train. Means one of you gents'll have to ride up on the front with me."

For this Haskins immediately volunteered.

When they went out into the early morning sunlight, baggage had already been loaded on the stage. There were three inside seats, each long enough for three people. Steve Mulgrave helped Christine Mayberry into the rear seat. Ron got in with them — not so much to be near the girl as to be less conspicuous himself. If he sat forward, those behind would be constantly looking at him. Two others were getting on here, and if they were people who'd lived in Prescott a year ago, one of them might recognize him. He was determined that there should be no exposure till he made it himself.

In a moment he saw that of the two who hadn't arrived by rail, one had already boarded the coach. Surprisingly she was a soft-cheeked Catholic nun in black cape and white headdress. She was on the front seat sitting between the Chinese restaurant man, Wan Sung, and Attorney Maxwell. As she chatted brightly with them, it was apparent that she knew them both quite well.

Christine gazed at her curiously. "But why," she wondered, "would she be at a place like this?"

Steve Mulgrave had the answer. "She's Mother Monica," he explained, "who runs the Sisters of St. Joseph Hospital at Prescott. When I went east with a beef shipment a coupla weeks ago, she was starting a tour of the grading camps. Lots of sick people in those camps — some of 'em with lead poisonin'. Sort of a ministering angel, you could call Mother Monica. Top of that she's an A-one doctor and nurse."

So now her tour of mercy was over and Mother Monica was heading back to her Prescott hospital. Ron had heard a good deal about railroad construction camps. There'd be one of them about every forty miles,

7

each a tough little tent city for the brief period that it was an important supply point, or railhead, or stagecoach swing station. There'd be plenty of gunplay at spots like that.

Right now he kept a sharp lookout for the other passenger due to get on here. A bare minute before they pulled out he emerged from a tent saloon and hurried toward the stage. A lean, swarthy man with black eyes and high cheekbones, wearing a checkered vest and with the tip of a gun holster showing beneath the skirt of his coat. At once Ron knew him. A year ago he'd stood face to face with him at the Exchange Saloon on Prescott's Whisky Row. The man had been dealing faro and for a few minutes Ron had stood idly by, watching the play. Twice later he'd passed the man on a plaza sidewalk.

There was only a slight chance that the gambler would recognize a fellow stage passenger, now with steel-rimmed glasses and a mustache, as a clear-eyed, clean-shaven, leather-jacketed range rider named Ron Garroway who'd crossed his path briefly a year ago. But just the same, Ron was glad that all inside seats were taken, which forced the man to join Haskins and the driver on the front boot. Wilkeson was his name.

A whip snapped and they were off, bumping westerly along ruts which paralleled the newly completed railroad grade. Steve Mulgrave spoke from the other side of Christine. "We'll change horses at Ingalls. Next after that'll be the noontime chuck stop — Flagstaff."

The first ten miles led due west across open grassland; then, looking out, Ron saw a fringe of timber ahead. When they came to it, it proved to be scrub cedar. The new grade of the A & P railbed continued on with no workmen in sight, this particular contractor having finished his quota. But dust from his grading slips still clung to the cedar boughs.

With each mile the cedars on either side grew higher. They were in an impressive juniper forest when, at mid-morning, Jake pulled up at the change station of Ingalls. There was no construction camp here; nothing but a stationmaster's cabin and a corral full of relay horses.

The change took just nine minutes. During them some of the passengers got off to stretch legs. Ron didn't. One who did was the gambler, Wilkeson. The man twirled a cigarette, then circled the coach glancing in curiously at his fellow passengers. Steve Mulgrave had also gotten off, and the gambler spoke to him. Both being from Prescott, they'd naturally know each other. Christine Mayberry had gotten off, and she moved forward to a group near a forewheel. Ron saw Frank Maxwell introduce her to Mother Monica.

Outside, Steve Mulgrave looked at Wilkeson's holster tip and it seemed to remind him of something. He came back to the coach and took a satchel out from under his seat. From this he took a gunbelt with a revolver hanging from it. "We're in gun country now," he said to Ron. "We've been averaging a stage holdup per month lately."

"You expect one on this trip?"

The ranch foreman shook his head. "But it won't hurt to be ready."

Four fresh horses were in the traces, and all but one of the passengers reboarded. The one was Wilkeson. He stood just outside Ron's window, looking in at him. His expression seemed half-puzzled, half-surprised. His cocked eye seemed to say, "Haven't I seen you before somewhere?"

The driver called him, and the man climbed up on the front box.

They were off at a trot along the south side of the roadbed. After a few more miles junipers gave way to tall, yellow-barked western pine. Christine looked out at snowy peaks showing above the trees. "It's beautiful!" she exclaimed. "Is it like this at Prescott?"

Ron of course couldn't answer. He'd already told her he'd never been in Prescott. Steve Mulgrave filled the void. "Quite a bit like this. Only our Prescott pines are mostly ponderosas instead of western yellow. It's high country there, just like here."

"How high?"

"Prescott's not quite six thousand feet up," Steve said. "But there's a nine-thousand-foot skyline just a few miles to the south."

Dust on the railroad grade ahead meant men and teams at work. Presently they came to a half-finished grade where skinners were moving dirt with slips and wheelers. "Welshmen," Steve explained. "First they tried Mexicans, then Chinese, then Irishmen. Lately they imported three thousand Welshmen, and 've got 'em strung out along the grades for the next two hundred miles west."

10

They passed a contractor's camp, then slowed to a walk to cross a shallow ravine. Workmen were throwing up a trestle there, and from off in the timber came the shrill rasp of a sawmill.

Ron's mind veered to Wilkeson. No use trying to avoid the man. They'd come face to face at meal stops. The next one would be Flagstaff, only an hour ahead. *If he points a finger*, Ron resolved firmly, *I'll admit nothing. Not till I get to the Prescott courthouse.*

Christine's face was turned from him as she talked to Steve. "Yes," she was saying wearily, "it's a long, hard trip. But not as long and as hard as my father took when he went to Prescott nine years ago."

Nine years ago, Ron calculated would be 1873.

"No railroad west of Kansas in those days," Mulgrave agreed, "except the Union Pacific across Wyoming and Utah to San Francisco."

"That was the way my father went," Christine said. "By train to San Francisco; there he took the steamship *Newbern*."

The foreman's interest quickened. "I've heard old-timers tell about the *Newbern*. Lots of people went to Arizona on her in seventy-three. They say it was an eighteen-hundred-mile voyage from Frisco down around the tip of Baja California, then up the Gulf to the mouth of the Colorado River."

"And then," Christine said, "Dad changed to a stern-wheel river steamer which carried him three hundred miles up the Colorado River, past Yuma and on to Ehrenburg. From there he had to ride a

11

stagecoach — really only a mud wagon — a hundred and seventy miles inland to Prescott."

So she was on her way, Ron concluded, to join her father, who now could be a prosperous merchant, stockman, or mine owner.

Steve Mulgrave had a puzzled look. "Don't recollect ever runnin' into anyone named Mayberry," he said, "around Prescott."

"You wouldn't be likely to." The girl looked from Steve to Ron and then spoke gravely to both of them. "A few weeks after he got there, nine years ago, my father disappeared."

And hasn't been seen since? Ron wanted to ask, but didn't. Neither did Steve. They were in a land where one didn't pry into the personal affairs of other people. Clearly this young girl's journey to Prescott had something to do with her father's disappearance there nine years ago. If she wanted to tell them about it, she would. They were to be coach companions for another twenty-four hours.

When the stage began slowing down, Lawyer Maxwell called back from the front seat. "Here we are. Flagstaff."

The place they were rolling into was half canvas and half raw, unpainted boards. Hammers pounded from a nearly finished depot going up beside the grade. Fronting a rutty street back of it were frame stores and saloons, with a hundred or more dwelling tents in sight. A forest of stately pines enclosed a settlement which showed promise of becoming a permanent town.

A Chinese in front of a shack restaurant was pounding a gong. As the driver stopped his stage he yelled, "Put on the feed bag, folks, while we change horses."

Minutes later the passengers were seated at a long, crude table, this one covered with oilcloth. Except for the addition of beans, food was the same as at breakfast. A Mexican woman collected fifty cents from each passenger.

Twice during the meal Ron saw Wilkeson staring at him. It was a narrow, knowing stare. *The worst he can do*, Ron thought, *is give me away a day too soon.*

He sat between Haskins and Rudd, who argued amicably about plans after reaching Prescott. Rudd wanted to open an assay office; Haskins wanted to spend the summer staking a placer claim and sluicing for gold on some nearby creek.

Christine was at the far end of the table between Maxwell and Mother Monica. As each diner finished, he or she went back to the coach. Wilkeson was one of the first to go; Ron made it a point to be last.

Just outside the door Wilkeson accosted him. An unlighted cigarette hung from the man's lower lip, and his eyes had a shrewd speculation. "Driver tells me your name's Andrews," he began bluntly.

"You any kin to a fella named Garroway who was in Prescott a year ago?"

"No. Why? Do I look like him?"

"You sure do." The man stood with a deadpan face waiting for Ron's response, like he might wait for someone to call a bet.

Ron decided grimly to see it through. "Who is this fella Garroway?" he asked.

"He's one of three masked men," Wilkeson said, "who held up the Prescott bank a year ago and shot a teller dead. They rode into the woods and separated. A posse caught two of 'em."

"And the other one?"

"He got clean away. But they know who he is all right. Name's Garroway and the two they caught told on him. Sheriff checked up and found that all three of 'em had been hangin' around together. One of 'em hit town with Garroway and took a room with him at the hotel. The two caught men had two-thirds of the loot on them. They figure Garroway got away because he hid his third in the woods so he could ride faster."

"What happened to the other men?"

Wilkeson, still with a deadpan face, held a match to his cigarette and blew rings. "They were tried, convicted, and hanged." He gave Ron a final narrow-eyed stare, then turned and went back to his seat on the stage.

CHAPTER
TWO

When the coach pulled out, Ron, Christine, and Steve Mulgrave again had the back seat together. The driver trotted his fresh horses for a mile, then pulled them to a walk. Here the trail was slightly upgrade with tall mountain timber on either side. They were climbing toward a minor divide, still paralleling what would soon be a railroad track. Graders were at work on a roadbed, and occasionally they passed bridge men putting up a trestle.

"How long have you lived near Prescott, Mr. Mulgrave?"

The girl's sudden question aroused Ron from his own disturbed thoughts, fixed absorbedly on Wilkeson. Not that what the gambler had told him was news to Ron. A newspaper account had informed him of a double hanging ten months ago on the courthouse lawn at Prescott.

"Call me Steve, please," Steve Mulgrave said. "Everybody else does. How long have I been out here? Only a couple of years. I'm strictly a stockman. Up to a coupla years ago everything around Prescott was mining. Now we have a few cattle and sheep outfits."

"So you couldn't have known my father."

15

"Not if he left Prescott in seventy-three. I hit there in the spring of eighty."

They rode a mile in silence. Then: "He was good at writing letters, Steve." Clearly she meant her long-lost father. Just as clearly she wanted to confide in the solidly intelligent ranch foreman who sat by her — and perhaps also in Ron, for when she went on she was speaking to them both. "He wrote my mother on the first three Saturday nights after he arrived. I was only thirteen then. The letters had to travel the same way he'd come himself, in reverse — stagecoach to the Colorado River, riverboat to salt water, steamship to San Francisco, and finally by rail to Ohio."

"Was it summertime or winter?" Steve asked.

"Summer. His first Prescott letter was postmarked July tenth, eighteen seventy-three; his next was postmarked July seventeenth; his third July twenty-fourth. I have them right here." She opened her purse and took out some very old letters.

Ron ventured a question. "Do they mention any trouble?"

"No. He said he liked Prescott. He said he was riding in all directions around the county, sometimes panning creek gravel for placer gold; sometimes chipping ledges for high-grade silver ore. As soon as he found what looked like a rich pocket or lode, he'd stake a claim."

"And nothing was heard from him after that third letter?"

"Not a word. My mother wrote frantically to the Prescott sheriff, who made a routine investigation. The report was that Adam Mayberry had bought a saddle horse and camp kit. Each Monday morning for three weeks he'd ridden into the hills, returning on Saturday night. He'd maintained a room over the Exchange Saloon on Montezuma Street. His extra clothes were still in it. He'd filed no claim. Nothing to indicate that he had or hadn't made a mineral strike. He was last seen at daybreak on Sunday, August first taking his horse out of Brooks's livery stable. No one noticed which direction he took from town . . . After a long search no trace could be found of him. The sheriff's conclusion was that Indians had killed him for his horse and saddle."

"The woods," Steve admitted ruefully, "were full of Indians in those days. Apaches, mostly. That was before General Crook rounded 'em up and put 'em on reservations."

"There was nothing my mother could do about it," Christine said. "She passed away two years ago, when I was twenty. Since then I've been teaching school in Cleveland."

For a while there was no sound except the clop-clop of hooves and the whir of wheels. Ron waited — sure that the girl's story had more to it. Why else now, two years after her mother's death and nine after her father's disappearance, would she be riding this stagecoach into the heart of Arizona?

He looked again at the letters she'd taken from her purse. There were four of them. One seemed to be a good deal more faded and soiled than the other three.

Christine followed his eyes and explained, beginning with a question for Steve. "How long since you left Prescott?"

"Nearly a month," he told her. "Had to drive those steers two hundred miles to Holbrook, then ship 'em by slow freight to Kaycee. Why? Did somethin' happen while I was gone?"

Christine nodded, her brown eyes turning first to Steve and then to Ron. "About ten days ago," she said, "two Skull Valley cowboys got caught in a hailstorm and took shelter in a shallow cave. There they found some slit-open mail sacks and an empty Wells Fargo express box. Registered letters had been opened and looted. Unregistered letters had simply been tossed aside. This is one of them."

She let them see an old, faded envelope addressed to her mother and postmarked at Prescott on July thirty-first, eighteen seventy-three. "The two cowboys took everything into town and gave it to the postmaster. He checked his records and found out that the mail stage leaving for Ehrenburg on Monday morning, August second, eighteen seventy-three, was held up and robbed near Skull Valley. The robbers were never caught."

Steve Mulgrave looked gravely at the old, salvaged letter. "Makes sense," he said. "Likely the robbers rode into the hills till their horses got winded; then they holed up in a cave for a while to rest and sort the loot."

"So the last letter my father wrote to my mother," Christine filled in, "lay unopened on that cave floor for nine years. The stamp was still on it, so it was still

18

deliverable. The Prescott postmaster forwarded it to me in Ohio with a note of his own explaining the delay."

What had happened seemed reasonably clear to Ron. On his fourth Saturday night in Prescott Mayberry had written the usual letter to his wife. He'd dropped it in the post office slot, gone to bed, and the next morning, Sunday, had again ridden out into the hills. He'd have no way of knowing that his fourth letter, due to go out on Monday's stage, would become waylaid by highwaymen.

"It gives you a lead," Ron suggested hopefully, "toward finding out what became of him?"

"Not a lead. Only a direction. It says that late during his third week of prospecting he found a rich silver ledge in the Bradshaw Mountains." The girl opened the long-lost letter to consult it again. "It was on the ridge between Milk Creek and Blind Indian Creek, south of Prescott. He staked a claim there, naming it the Newbern after the ship which had brought him to Arizona. With a sackful of samples he rode back to Prescott, getting there late Saturday to find the filing office closed till Monday. All three assay offices were also closed. So he went to the home of one of the three assayers and left the sample sack with him. In his room he wrote the letter to my mother, mailed it before he went to bed. We now know that early Sunday morning he took his horse out of Brooks's livery stable. We don't know why. Perhaps he rode back to his claim to check the filing stakes he'd driven at the four corners of it."

Steve asked alertly, "Did he say which of the three assayers he left the sample with?"

"No. The name would have meant nothing to my mother. But in the letter my father said he was sure the sample would assay better than a thousand dollars worth of silver per ton of ore. He was a trained metallurgist himself."

Steve brooded over it a minute. "A sample that rich," he concluded, "might start a rush for the Milk Creek ridge. Maybe the assayer kept it under his hat with the idea of going there himself alone. What I want to know is, why didn't he come forward and tell about the sample left with him when your father turned up missing?"

"That's exactly," Christine answered, "what I'm going there to find out."

"People come and go at Prescott," Steve said. "Not likely that those same three assayers are still doing business there, after nine years."

Again the girl opened her purse and this time brought out the folded front page of an old newspaper. It was from the Prescott weekly *Miner* with a date in August, 1873. "The sheriff sent it to us during the search for my father. It gives the story of the search and suggests that Apaches were responsible for his disappearance. My mother kept it with these letters."

Steve looked at the old account and shook his head. "Nothing here you haven't told us."

He passed the paper to Ron, who noticed that the left-hand column was made up of advertising cards. All the 1873 professional men of Prescott were listed there. Two doctors, four lawyers, one surveyor, three assayers. Ron read aloud the names of the three assayers:

"Wimpole, Vrooman, Rood. Any of them still there, Steve?"

"Only Wimpole. Vrooman and Rood were gone by the time I hit town."

Ron looked at the names of the four advertising lawyers. He'd be needing a lawyer himself within an hour after showing his face at Prescott. The four who'd placed cards in the 1873 paper were Coles Bashford, H. E. Carttier, J. P. Hargrave, and Frank Maxwell. So Maxwell was one of the old-timers! Should he retain Maxwell, or one of the others? A whir of wheels and a thud of hooves made him aware that an east-bound coach was passing them, on its way to the Canyon Diablo railhead.

Shortly after three o'clock they changed horses at a station called Parker. Everyone got out to stretch during the ten-minute stop. Ron kept an appraising eye on Frank Maxwell and was close by when Parker, the station man, hailed him. "Hi, Frank. How far east did you go this trip?"

"Only to Kansas City, Park. Had to explain some papers to a client there before I could get him to sign 'em."

"Took you a long time, didn't it? It's been two weeks since you went through here on your way east."

It struck Ron that the lawyer answered overcautiously and in a tone of alert defense. "Lots of bright lights in Kaycee, Park. Stayed over a few days to take 'em in."

The words were natural and convincing. Only the tone seemed cautious, strained, defensive. Ron decided

21

to reserve judgment on Maxwell till further observation.

They continued on with four fresh horses, still through a pine forest, now on a descending trail on the north side of the railroad roadbed. During the next hour Christine slept briefly. Not to disturb her, Steve and Ron refrained from talk. Ron had a few questions he wanted to ask Steve, but they could wait. Maybe Steve would recommend a Prescott lawyer.

Christine didn't waken till the stop at Pittman. Again there was nothing but a corral full of relay horses and a cabin office. The contractor on this section of roadbed had finished his work and was gone.

"Plenty of people at the next stop," Steve said as the coach moved on. "Bill Williams Mountain." He pointed obliquely ahead out of a south window to a high, timbered peak. "Be dark time we get there. Supper stop at eight o'clock. Understand they've dropped part of the name and are callin' the place Williams."

"Why is it important?" Ron asked.

"It'll be a division point, for one thing. So a lot of speculators came in to buy lots. Two or three of the biggest construction contractors make it a headquarters and supply point. More 'n six hundred people there already."

The sun went down behind Bill Williams Mountain, and the cool of twilight came on. At exactly eight o'clock Jake rattled his coach into Williams, which already boasted more than a score of plank stores and saloons. Carpenters had finished a depot which was twice the size of the one at Flagstaff. Construction was under way on a roundhouse and water tank. Acres of tents housed workers and boomers. One of the front street saloons was two stories, and in an upper window Ron saw the bold, painted face of a woman. "Toughest town on the grade," Steve said as they walked with Christine to the eating place. "Next one's almost as bad. Simms' Camp. They're building a long tunnel near there."

Christine left them to join Mother Monica. Inside, Ron chose a seat across from Frank Maxwell. "How do you like Arizona by now, Andrews?" the lawyer asked jovially. He was the least jaded of the passengers. The man had shaved on the train, and his tailor-made suit had miraculously kept its press.

"It's a fine-looking country," Ron said.

"And full of fine people," Maxwell added, "except at these mushroom towns along the grade. Here you'll find riffraff — anything from footpads to prostitutes. Will you be in Prescott long?"

"My future," Ron evaded, "isn't definite."

"That's a mighty pretty girl you're riding with. Wouldn't want to trade seats, would you?"

Ron didn't answer, mainly because he could see the gambler Wilkeson again bending a speculative look his way. He finished hurriedly and went back to his seat on the stage.

At half past eight they were on their way again, bumping along a downgrade toward Simms' Camp. The moist, tangy smell of snowbound pine trees came to them from the summit of Bill Williams Mountain. By nine o'clock it was pitch dark, and again Christine slept briefly. Ron looked at her small, tired face, not six inches from his own shoulder. Frank Maxwell was right — she was a mighty pretty girl. He'd wanted to change seats with Ron. Was he a single man? Ron wondered.

Again Steve and Ron sat silent in the dark, careful not to waken the girl. She awoke of her own accord just as they got to Simms' Camp. Or perhaps the pace jolted her awake, for they arrived at a gallop. A new driver had taken over at Williams.

He pulled up in front of the change station. "Why do we stop so often?" Christine asked.

"We have to have fresh horses," Steve told her, "every fifteen miles or so. That's about every two and a half hours."

Since she had been asleep, the time had passed quickly for her. Now it lacked only an hour of midnight. A stage company man called out an announcement. "Free coffee in the station, folks. You got ten minutes."

Nearly everyone went for coffee, if only to break the monotony. The station house had a noisy tent saloon on either side of it. Boisterous talk came from them, and Ron could imagine the backwash of the frontier in there. A hundred tunnel workers and graders took their fun here, and there'd be predatory men and women to prey on them. In the stage house they found a wood stove with a steaming pot on it. Mother Monica was pouring coffee. There was no place to sit down. As Ron looked around, he saw Wilkeson but failed to see Maxwell.

"Where's Frank?" someone asked. "Didn't he get off?"

The white-capped nun answered. "He's asleep and I couldn't bear to waken him. Here you are, my dear." She handed Christine a tin of coffee.

Mother Monica took none herself. As usual, she was here only to serve others. She was the first to return to the coach, and one of the hostlers, who'd just traced up four fresh horses, guided her to it.

As he handed her into the dark vehicle the others heard her cry of dismay. "Mr. Maxwell! What happened?" She turned to alert those coming behind her. "He was attacked in the dark! Struck down and robbed, I think. Please bring a light."

Everyone crowded up to the coach, peering in. Ever since Canyon Diablo the front seat had been occupied by Wan Sung, Mother Monica, and Maxwell. Only the lawyer had been in the coach these last nine minutes. In the flare of a hostler's lantern the man seemed to be stunned or dead. He was slumped over as though he'd been clouted with a club or the barrel of a gun. Mother Monica, a competent nurse and healer, was now in there with him.

"He's alive, praise the Lord," she reported, "but in no condition to continue on. He must be kept here at least till tomorrow's stage. I'll stay with him myself. Will you please bring a cot, or a stretcher of some kind?"

Ron looked around at the two tent saloons, each swarming with ruffians. Evidently some footpad or camp thug had come out of one of those dives to find the stage empty except for one sleeping passenger. A prosperous-looking passenger who could have a fat wallet. Circling to the darker side of the coach, he'd knocked the sleeper senseless in order to rifle his pockets.

While they were taking Maxwell out of the stage, Ron went around to the far side for a look. A wallet lay on the ground there. The only thing left in it was Frank Maxwell's professional card. After stripping money from it, the thief had thrown the wallet away.

CHAPTER
THREE

When Ron returned to the lantern-lighted side of the coach, he found Maxwell lying on a canvas cot. A moist towel was across his forehead, and Mother Monica was chafing his wrists. The man's eyes opened with a glassy stare as he came slowly out of a stupor.

"What about givin' him a shot of this?" Wilkeson offered. The gambler brought a whisky flask from his pocket. Mother Monica made no objection when he held it to Maxwell's lips.

"This is empty," Ron told the nun as he handed her the wallet. "Found it on the other side of the coach."

"So are his pockets," Steve Mulgrave added. "Not a dime left on him."

When consciousness returned to the victim, Steve asked him, "Did you see who he was?"

"I was asleep," the lawyer answered faintly.

"He can have my bed," the station man offered, "if you want to rest him here till the next stage."

Wan Sung and the stage driver picked up the cot, with Maxwell on it, and carried it like a litter into the station. Some of the others, including Christine, followed them. Steve Mulgrave and the two hostlers went to the noisiest of the tent saloons to ask the bartender and customers there who had and hadn't been in sight during the first nine minutes after the stage's arrival.

Ron went only as far as the front room of the station house. There he borrowed a lantern and went back to the coach. He circled it to the spot where he'd found the empty wallet. It was a weedy place and quite dark except for the glow of his lantern. All the tents and shacks here at Simms' Camp were on the station side of the trail.

Maybe the thief had thrown away something else, or maybe dropped something of his own. Ron flashed his lantern about, searching the ground there. In a minute he saw a small rectangle of blue in the weeds. It looked like a tiny booklet. A memo book which Maxwell had carried? Such a thing would be worthless to the thief, so he had probably thrown it away.

Ron picked it up and saw that it was a bank's passbook. What surprised him was that it had been issued by a bank in St. Louis, Missouri. It was a savings account. The depositor was Frank Maxwell, and the account had been opened just four days ago. There'd been a single deposit in the sum of twenty-three thousand dollars.

Which proved that four days ago Maxwell had been in St. Louis. Since then there'd been just time enough for him to ride a train to Kansas City and there catch a Santa Fe train to an end-of-track in Arizona where he could connect with this stage for Prescott.

Then Ron remembered a question Maxwell had answered at the Parker station. How far east had he gone this trip? Only to Kansas City, he'd answered. Why had he lied? His manner had been cautious, strained, defensive. Why had he denied a side trip to St. Louis?

Ron spent another minute looking for anything else which might have been dropped or thrown away by a footpad. He found nothing.

When he went back to the station house, the front room was empty. An open door gave on the station man's living quarters, and he found Maxwell on a bed there. Mother Monica sat by him, insisting that he remain quietly here till tomorrow's stage. Christine, Dan McCurdy, and the station man were there. Maxwell, pale and in evident pain, lay with his eyes closed.

Ron showed them the bank passbook. McCurdy reached for it, looked at it curiously. "The thief threw it away," Ron explained, "along with the wallet."

Frank Maxwell heard and opened his eyes. He saw the little blue book and something like fright showed in his eyes. "Let me have it." He held out his hand, and his fingers closed tightly on the book, hiding it from sight. Ron had a feeling that the twenty-three-thousand-dollar deposit in a faraway city might be the key to some sinister secret. The man on the bed started to say something, then clamped his lips. He didn't even thank Ron.

"Where's Steve?" Ron asked.

The others didn't know, so he left to find out. Outside he ran into the stage driver, who was fretting to get started. His horses were traced and he was already half an hour late.

Mulgrave, he told Ron, had decided to lay over here a day for two reasons. To join a search party now being organized by the saloon owners and the tunnel foreman; they'd search every tent at Simms' Camp for loot taken from Maxwell. And to help Mother Monica take care of Maxwell and conduct him on to Prescott by the next stage. "It'll be a ten-man search party. Couple of straw bosses and a bartender'll join it. Ain't likely to find anything. The guy's had time to bury his take by now."

Ron didn't see Steve again. The search party was already moving from tent to tent, flashing lanterns in the dark. After an hour the stage driver was able to pull out. Haskins and Wilkeson no longer needed to ride on the driver's boot. They took the inside seats vacated by Maxwell and Mother Monica. And since Steve had remained behind at Simms' Camp, Ron and Christine had the dark rear seat to themselves.

Clouds covered the mountain sky as the coach moved on. It was a starless midnight with the breakfast stop, Chino Valley, still two stations away.

Ron could barely see Christine sitting in the dark at his elbow. She'd slept twice, so wasn't likely to sleep again after the excitement at Simms' Camp. People in the forward seats were talking about it, but Ron couldn't make out words above the rumble of wheels.

He barely heard Christine when she asked, "Why don't you get some sleep yourself, Mr. Andrews?"

30

The name grated on him, even shamed him. Mulgrave had asked her to call him Steve — but the man she was riding with now couldn't ask her to call him by any name at all. The only one she knew was a false one. A rebellion against it gripped Ron. Why not tell her the truth? She'd find it out anyway, and so would everyone else, an hour or so after arrival at Prescott.

Since she was certain to hear his story before this new day was over, he wanted her to hear it from his own lips. On an impulse he began telling it, keeping his voice low. "What would you think if I told you my name isn't Andrews?"

When she didn't answer, he went on with a rush of words, impatient to get it over with. "My name's Garroway and there's a warrant out for me at Prescott. They've been hunting for me for a year. I'm going there to give myself up."

Her shocked whisper came from the dark. "I can't believe it!"

"Please believe one other thing," he begged. "I didn't do the thing I'm charged with."

"It happened a year ago?" The thump of wheels covered her breathless question.

"Just a year ago. Do you want to hear about it?"

"Yes. Tell me."

Some warm quality in her voice helped him to go on. He told her he'd been raised on a Midwest stock farm and had spent a season herding cattle in Colorado. "Then an uncle died and left me a little money, so I figured to go further west and start a cow ranch of my

31

own. I'd heard about good grass and an uncrowded range in Arizona. So I headed this way; took a Southern Pacific train to Tucson and from there went on by stagecoach to Prescott. That was in May of eighty-one, before the Santa Fe had any rails west of Albuquerque."

"Did you know anyone in Prescott?"

"Nobody except the people who rode in on the stage with me. Just like you'll know only me and Steve and Mother Monica when you get there. My chance seatmate on the stage was a stranger named Crocker. Only one hotel at Prescott, the Williams House, and only one vacant room when Crocker and I walked in, so we shared it together. He said he was a wool buyer. In the morning we went down to the dining room and had breakfast together. Then I bought a horse and a light camp kit and began scouting the range; wanted to get an idea about where to file or buy land."

When he got back to town, Ron told her, he found Crocker and another man eating supper. "Not knowing anyone else, I joined them. Other man said he was Gus Stallings. Twice later that week I was seen eating with Crocker and Stallings. Once they took me into the Palace Saloon for a beer. Then I was off on another three-day scouting trip, looking for a spot to start a cow ranch."

Christine's mind leaped ahead of him. "And something happened while you were gone?"

"You guessed it. Three masked men held up the Prescott bank; shot a teller and got away with sixty thousand dollars. Out in the hills they split the take three ways and each went a different direction. Posses chased them. Two were caught; one wasn't. Twenty thousand dollars was found on each of the captured men. Without their masks they were recognized as Crocker and Stallings. The sheriff tried to make them name the third man. At first they wouldn't. Then people remembered having seen them with me. They found out that Crocker and I had come in on the stage together, that we'd shared a room; I'd been seen eating and drinking with both Crocker and Stallings."

"But that," Christine protested, "didn't really prove anything."

"Not till the sheriff asked them. 'What about that man Garroway you've been hangin' around with?' It gave them a lead. They had nothing to lose by naming me, and everything to gain. It would let their partner get safely away with twenty thousand dollars. Maybe he'd use some of it to hire them a lawyer; or if they escaped, they might join him and collect. Made no difference what happened to me. So they said, yes, the third man was Garroway. Then up popped a warrant for my arrest on a charge of bank robbery and murder."

"How awful!" The girl's whisper came breathlessly from the dark. "And you didn't even know about it?"

"Not till my third night out when I stopped to buy bacon at a small store on the Verde River, forty miles east of Prescott. A late copy of the Prescott paper was on the counter. My name in headlines! I'd been tabbed by Crocker and Stallings as their partner in a bank murder. Posses were out after me. I panicked and rode east into the Mogollons. For the next week I holed up by daylight and rode by night. Finally made it back to

33

Colorado and took a ranch job under the name of Andrews."

It was a long time before Christine said anything. Darkness masked her face, and there was no way to tell whether she believed him.

"So after a year," she said finally, "you're back to give yourself up. But isn't it just as dangerous now as it was then?"

"Not quite," Ron thought. "That newspaper I'd seen in the store mentioned lynch talk. The bank teller had been popular, and the town was plenty mad. It's been a year now — long enough for hotheads to cool a little. I'm tired of running, hiding, telling lies about my name. And the case against me isn't as tight as it was against Crocker and Stallings. They were caught with two-thirds of the loot in their saddlebags."

"That should make a difference," the girl agreed. "Have you told anyone else besides me?"

"No. I was thinking I'd tell you and Mulgrave together some time during the night. But he left us at Simms' Camp. I'll need a lawyer, and I thought maybe Steve would recommend one."

"I'll perhaps need one too," Christine said. "I was going to ask Steve about Mr. Maxwell."

"So was I," Ron said. But he'd changed his mind now. All he knew about Frank Maxwell was that he'd lied about going farther east than Kansas City, and had seemed frightened by the exposure of a twenty-three-thousand-dollar bank deposit in St. Louis.

"Did you ever find out," Christine asked, "what happened to Crocker and Stallings?"

"They were convicted and hanged," he told her. He heard the shocked catch of her breath as the Prescott stage jolted on.

CHAPTER
FOUR

In the middle seat the saloonman McCurdy said something to Rudd. Ron, directly behind them, failed to catch the words. It made him fairly sure that his own confidence to Christine hadn't been overheard.

"Do you believe me?"

"Yes." The promptness of the affirmative was comforting.

"Do you think I'm right in giving myself up?"

This time she waited a minute. Even then her response seemed uncertain. "Yes . . . but I wish you wouldn't."

"When I first made up my mind," Ron said, "I went to the nearest sheriff's office. The sheriff was out and I had to wait. When he came in he had a prisoner in handcuffs. Then I knew what would happen if I told him I'm wanted at Prescott."

"What would he have done?"

"He'd hold me in jail and telegraph the Prescott sheriff, who'd send a deputy to get me. The deputy would take me back in handcuffs — by train and stage all the way from Lamar, Colorado, to Prescott, Arizona. I'd be sitting by him right now with my wrist linked to his. This way, going by myself, I have a little dignity —

a chance to make a friend or two like you and Steve Mulgrave."

Suddenly her small hand reached from the dark and took his own. "It's better this way," she agreed.

Yes, Ron thought, a thousand times better than a manacle, that soft touch of a friend's hand. Only for a minute the hand was there, and then was gone.

When they stopped to change horses at Partridge Creek, it was four o'clock and still dark. During the halt no one got off. Maybe the others were thinking about what had happened to Maxwell at Simms' Camp. For the rest of this dark night no one wanted to be apart from company, on or off the coach.

In the quiet of the stop Ron heard talk from forward seats. "We've left the railroad now," McCurdy was telling Rudd. Prescott, he explained, was sixty miles south of the rail route which was heading westerly toward a crossing of the Colorado River at Needles.

The man Conway, sharing the middle seat with Rudd and McCurdy, was asleep.

Fresh animals were traced and the coach moved on, the route bending due south now. "Try for another nap," Ron urged the girl.

Whether she did or not he couldn't tell. For the next hour she was quiet, and then dawn light began filtering in. As it brightened, Ron saw that they were now in an open valley well to the west of Bill Williams Mountain. No sign of a railroad grade. Even after the railroad was in operation, Prescott people would need to ride a stage sixty miles to reach it.

When it was broad light, Christine took off her bonnet and brought a comb from her purse. Combing her hair, she said ruefully, "I feel messy and jaded, like my mouth's full of cotton. Do they have bathtubs at the Prescott hotel?"

"Only one. You wait your turn. A year ago it was the only hotel in town and probably still is: the Williams House on Gurley Street."

"You were at the Williams House a year ago," Christine remembered. "So they'll know you, won't they, when you walk in?"

"For that reason," Ron decided, "I won't go in there. I need an hour to clean up before I go to the sheriff's office. I'll hunt me up a rooming house on another side of the plaza."

At seven o'clock they made the breakfast stop at Chino Valley. It was a small trading settlement with a store-saloon-hotel. Sheds at the rear had stacks of last year's hay on them. The atmosphere was peaceful, homespun, in marked contrast to the rough-tough camps along the rail grade.

It was much the same at the midmorning stop — a place called Twenty Mile Station run by a man named Delaney. And again at a lunch stop where the stage arrived at one p.m. "Thirty minutes to eat," the driver called. "We're an hour late, so don't keep me waiting."

The station man's wife put a kindly arm around Christine. "Don't let him rush you, my dear. I'm Sara Banghart. You must be tired to death, riding day and night with all those men. Come with me if you'd like to freshen up a bit." She led Christine away to her own room.

Ron, heading toward the dining room, suddenly found Wilkeson at his elbow. "I just thought of somethin'," the man said. "Somethin' you oughta know. Better see me a minute before we pull out. Last chance you'll get. Next stop's Prescott."

The gambler turned abruptly away, and while they were eating he didn't even look toward Ron. *He's made up his mind. He's sure about me now. He knows I'm Garroway.*

That being the case, what did the man have up his sleeve? What could he gain by having a private word with Ron at this last stop on the road?

Did he want a bribe for not giving Ron away? That threat would have no teeth, because Ron would already have exposed himself. An hour after arrival he'd walk into the courthouse and identify himself as a wanted man.

Yet sheer curiosity impelled him to find out what was on Wilkeson's mind. There'd be nothing to lose by it. He left the table ten minutes before the others and went out to stand by a pulley well near the corrals. Hostlers were changing the stage horses. Looking south across the great basin which held Prescott, Ron could see the high, pine-clad skyline of the Bradshaw Mountains.

Almost at once Wilkeson appeared and joined him.

"You're Garroway," he said bluntly. "Don't try to fool me anymore. I've been sizing you up ever since Canyon Diablo."

"Suppose I am. What about it?"

"You'll be eatin' your next meal in a cell," Wilkeson said. "Whether they hang you or not, like they did Crocker and Stallings, could depend a good deal on a witness named Wally Merton."

"Who's Wally Merton?" It was a name Ron had never heard before.

"He's a night bartender at one of the Whiskey Row saloons. The night before the bank robbery three men came in for drinks. It was after midnight, and there were no other customers. Wally served them. Two of them were Crocker and Stallings."

"And the third man?"

"Maybe he was you. Maybe he wasn't. Only Wally Merton can say yes or no."

At once Ron caught what it could mean for him. A main count against him was that he'd hobnobbed around town with Crocker and Stallings. As far as the law knew, he was the *only* one who'd associated with that pair. Now it seemed that only a few hours before the bank robbery they'd had drinks with another man. So if in court the barman Merton looked at him and said, "No, he's not the third of three men I served that night," then half the prosecution's case would go down the drain.

"Where," Ron asked, "can I find Wally Merton?"

"He won't go on duty till eight o'clock," Wilkeson said. "We'll hit town about four, and you could see him at his house — if you're quick and don't let the law pick you up first."

At once Ron decided to do just that. "Where does he live?"

"Know where the corner of Carleton and Marina is? Wally lives in a green clapboard cottage on the southeast corner. Likely he sleeps all morning and half the afternoon. Ought to be getting up about the time the stage pulls in."

"Thanks. I'll look him up as soon as we hit town."

Ron went to his stage seat half hopeful and half confused. As far as he could see there was nothing to be lost by looking up the bartender. The man would either say he was or say he wasn't one of a trio of customers. If he told the truth, it would go a long way toward winning Ron's acquittal. Maybe he could even persuade the man to go with him to the courthouse. They could walk into the sheriff's office; Ron could say, "I'm Ron Garroway"; and the witness could say, "But he's not the man I saw with Crocker and Stallings, trading treats, only a little while before the bank job."

When all passengers had boarded the coach, the driver whipped his new team to a run toward Arizona's territorial capital. Ron had an impulse to tell Christine about Wally Merton. Yet maybe he'd better wait till he'd seen the man. After a year Merton might be undecided or indefinite about the identification. And what about Wilkeson? Why had he gone out of his way to pass on the tip about Merton? He didn't look like a man who'd help a stranger out of the goodness of his heart.

He'd see Merton first, Ron decided. The corner where he lived was only a ten-minute walk from the plaza.

41

As the coach wheeled along, he looked out on a familiar range of black grama grass. Just a year ago he'd scouted this area; that house and corral layout off to his left, he remembered, was the Jan Rees ranch. He'd stopped there to water his horse.

Farther on they rattled past the Shivers farm with a plowed field back of it. A sun-bonneted woman stood at the gate to wave at the driver.

As each mile slipped by, a tension grew in Ron. By the look on her face he knew that Christine was sharing it with him. "I wish," she worried, "that you'd see a lawyer before giving yourself up."

"Maybe I will," Ron said. He'd have about two hours between arrival and the closing of offices at six o'clock. Time enough to see Wally Merton, then a lawyer. Maybe he could get both Merton and the lawyer to go with him to the courthouse.

Cattle grazing near the trail had a big CB on their flanks. "Campbell and Baker stuff," he told Christine, mainly to get her mind, and his own, off what lay ahead at Prescott.

Another hour and they crossed Willow Creek at the Stevens ranch. Then over a rise and down into Granite Creek at a grotto-like formation of limestone called the Dells. From here the trail followed Granite Creek, which had a fringe of cottonwood and willows.

Long, orderly rows of wooden barracks came in sight. They could see a military headquarters with a flagstaff in front. Soldiers were drilling on a parade ground. "Fort Whipple," Ron said.

"My father spoke of it in a letter," Christine remembered. "He said it was started in eighteen sixty-three, ten years before he came here himself."

From Fort Whipple to the Prescott Plaza was only a mile. They rattled down a lane of log cabins, whirled into Gurley Street, which made one side of a big rectangular plaza with a brick courthouse in its center. Saloons lined the west side of the plaza almost solidly, while stores, restaurants, livery stables, and small shops with only an occasional bar lined the other three sides. A big brick store on the north side had the name Bashford over it. A dozen young cottonwood trees had been planted on the courthouse lawn, and a gang of jail prisoners herded by a shotgun deputy formed a bucket brigade carrying water to them. Wagons and saddle mounts stood at the hitchrails. The high board sidewalks had gaps wherever there was a vacant lot or a small shabby shop. The driver made his last hundred yards at a gallop, pulling up in front of a two-story frame building on the northwest corner of Gurley and Cortez Streets. "End of the line," he yelled.

A sign on the building said:

THE WILLIAMS HOUSE
Board — $8 per Week
Single meals — 50¢

As they got out of the coach, Christine looked at it in dismay. "It's the best there is," Ron told her. "Food isn't too bad. Tomorrow maybe you can get a room in some private home."

43

"You're not coming in?"

"No. Fred Williams or his clerk might recognize me. Don't want to be told on; a lot better if I tell on myself."

The driver took baggage from the rear boot and set it on the walk. A Mexican porter came out and took Christine's. As Ron picked up his own bag, she held out her hand. "Good luck, Ron. Please send word if there's anything I can do."

"You can tell Steve about me when he comes in tomorrow." He forced a grin as he looked across at the bucket brigade of jailbirds on the courthouse lawn. "He'll likely find me helping those fellows pack water."

He saw a hurt in the girl's eyes, and before she could say anything else he hurried diagonally across the intersection and struck Cortez Street in front of Sol Lewis's Bank of Arizona. It was a minute after four o'clock and the bank had closed for the day.

He walked quickly along this east side of the plaza, which was the side with the fewest saloons and the most imposing stores. People along the walk looked at him curiously, but he counted on his steel-rimmed glasses and mustache to escape recognition. He went by a big brick store with the name Morris Goldwater over it. Then past a gunshop and an assayer's office. Another big store in the block had the name Buffum over it.

Near the end of the block Ron found what he wanted. A frame building with the sign: *Mrs. G. Johnson — Rooms by Day or Week.*

The ground floor was a bakeshop, and Ron took steep, narrow steps to an upper hall. It was empty, but when he rang a bell a woman appeared. "Just in on the stage?" she asked. In his businessman's topcoat, she may have taken him for a salesman with a prejudice against the Williams House.

He nodded. "I'd like your best room and a pan of hot water."

When she made him register, he signed "A. Andrews," thankful that it was the last time he'd need to use that name. After she'd shown him the room, he paid her for one night. The hot water came and he shaved carefully, but kept the mustache. He didn't want to be seen without it till he'd delivered himself to the law.

It took about thirty minutes to shave, bathe, change his shirt, and polish his boots. He must look his best when he faced the courthouse people.

Leaving his bag and topcoat in the room, he went down to the street. A few steps south along it took him to the Goodwin Street corner, where Hovey's Hall reminded him that a year ago the place had served alternately as a theater, a church, and a ballroom.

Here he turned east and walked a long uphill block to Marina Street. When he headed south on Marina, he was out of the business district. Only small dwellings lay beyond here. There was no sidewalk. It was another long block to Carleton Street, and on the southeast corner there Ron saw a green clapboard cottage, just where Wilkeson said it would be.

It was a shabby little house. The yard fence had broken pickets and the front gate hung askew on one hinge. An unmarried night bartender who used the

45

house only for a daytime sleeping place wouldn't be likely to keep it in good order.

Ron went to its door and had to knock twice before he heard someone coming. The man who opened the door had a heavy red face and a bullish build. His hair was rumpled like he'd just gotten out of bed. He might well be a night bartender on Whiskey Row.

"Are you Wally Merton?" Ron asked him.

"That's me. Whatta yuh want?"

"I'd like to see you a minute."

"Aw right, come on in."

Not till Ron had stepped inside did he see that something was wrong. This front room was completely unfurnished. Almost at once the look on the man's face changed. Instead of being heavy and dull it became crafty. Already he'd closed the door and stood with his back to it.

His eyes squinted slyly. "Welcome to Prescott, Garroway. And don't try to kid me about why you came back." He raised his voice. "Ernie, come on out and take a look. He walked right into the trap."

A second man appeared from a back room with a double-barreled shotgun. This one was a flyweight, thin-boned, sharp-faced.

"He's lookin' for someone named Wally Merton," the first man jeered. "Know anybody by that name, Ernie?"

"Never heard of him," Ernie said. "How 'bout you, Buck?"

"I never heard of him either, Ernie. Must be some name Monte made up." Both men laughed. But Ron was still more chagrined than alarmed. His first

46

thought was that there might be a reward posted for him and that these two roughs, along with Wilkeson, had schemed to collect it. "Monte" could be a nickname for Wilkeson.

"I'm on my way to the courthouse," Ron told them, "to give myself up."

Again they laughed. "Everybody believes that," Ernie said, "stand on his head."

"You're a cinch to get hanged," Buck said, "if you let 'em know you're Garroway. Only one thing could bring you back here. Twenty thousand dollars! You stashed it in the wood a year ago. Tomorrow you can show us the place and we'll help you dig it up."

It made the coup clear to Ron. Men like these, and like Wilkeson, couldn't conceive of his coming back here for any purpose except to recover buried loot. He'd need only to stay away from the courthouse for one night, then early tomorrow rent a horse and ride off into the forest where he'd disappeared a year ago. This time there'd be no one chasing him. He could dig up the money at his leisure and head out of the country. No other routine would make sense to men like Ernie, Buck, and Wilkeson.

In the thirty minutes it had taken Ron to shave, bathe, and change, Wilkeson must have planted these roughs in this vacant house. And since there was no such person as night bartender Wally Merton, there'd be no such person as a third man seen at a bar with Crocker and Stallings some ten hours before last year's bank robbery.

Could he fight his way out? Nothing would be lost by trying. Ernie would hardly dare to use the shotgun because the nearest occupied cottage was less than sixty yards away. A gunshot would be heard and reported.

A litter of trash in a corner of the room showed an empty whiskey bottle. With a quick movement Ron snatched it up. "I'm walking out on you," he told them, and took a step toward Buck, whose back was still to the door.

Ernie swung his shotgun to an aim. "They'll be pickin' birdshot outa yuh," he warned, "for the next coupla months."

"I'd still be better off than I am now." Clubbing his bottle and seeming to ignore Ernie, Ron took another step toward Buck.

The beefy Buck was in a half crouch, waiting for him. His elbows were bent, his clawed hands ready. One more step and Ron was almost within his reach. Then he turned and threw the bottle hard into Ernie's face.

The shock dropped Ernie to his knees with a yell. For a breath it drew Buck's eyes that way, and at the same instant Ron made a head-first dive at his stomach. As Buck doubled up his flailing arms missed Ron. The door was only a step away and Ron staggered to it. His hand was on the knob when Ernie recovered and came at him with the shotgun, crashing the barrel on his head.

He didn't remember falling. When he came to, he was on a back room cot, feet tied and mouth gagged. Somewhere in the scuffle his steel-rimmed glasses had been knocked off. Voices reached him as he came groggily out of a fog.

"Is the wagon ready, Ernie?"

"It's out back, Buck. After dark we can haul him out to the Groom Crik shack. We'll work on him there."

"A helluva lot o' trouble," Buck complained, "just to split twenty thousand three ways with Monte."

"Beats muckin' rock in a mine," Ernie countered, "at three dollars a day. You keep an eye on him while I go down to the Row for some likker."

"If you see Monte, tell him everything worked out fine."

CHAPTER
FIVE

Christine slept late at the Williams House. Her bed wasn't what she was used to, but after thirty-three hours on a stagecoach any bed was luxury. It was too late for breakfast. All other occupants had gone out for the day, which allowed her to take a bath without waiting in line. When she went down to the lobby she found Fred Williams himself at the desk.

He rang for a waitress, who brought Christine a pot of coffee. With it and this morning's *Miner* she went back to her room. The room had a washstand and a threadbare carpet. Her first thought was of Ron Garroway, and she looked anxiously at the front page headlines. If a man long wanted for murder had given himself up, it would be in the news.

It wasn't. Why? Had he changed his mind? How could she find out?

Steve Mulgrave would be in on the next stage, due at three this afternoon. She needed Steve's advice in regard to her own nine-year-old mystery. But that could wait. No immediate crisis was involved there. With Ron it was different. She knew that he would have included Steve in his back-seat confidence if the ranch foreman hadn't left the stage at Simms' Camp. So she decided to pass Ron's story on to Steve when he came in this afternoon. A discreet inquiry at the courthouse by Steve would let them know whether Ron had, or hadn't, surrendered to the law.

Propped on the bed with a pillow at her back, Christine skimmed through today's local paper. It told her that a man named Tritle was governor of Arizona Territory. It mentioned that cattle had been mysteriously disappearing out toward the head of the Hassayampa. Editorially the *Miner* hinted that a few lynchings would cure the situation.

The name "Blind Indian Creek" caught Christine's eye. She remembered that her father's long-lost letter said that he'd made a rich strike on a ridge between Blind Indian and Milk Creeks. So she read the news item which contained the name.

Six more bars of bullion came in yesterday from Chad Granby's Skyline mine on the ridge above Blind Indian Creek. They weigh out at $12,677.50. What are you going to do with all that money, Chad?

How far was the Skyline, Christine wondered, from a claim called the Newbern which was staked but never filed? Who was the assayer with whom her father had left an ore sample nine years ago? And why had he kept quiet during the search for Adam Mayberry?

She looked for another mention of Blind Indian Creek but found none. Wild turkey, the paper said, were plentiful along the Agua Fria. Much of the paper was advertisements. One of them read:

GO EAST; ride a CONCORD coach to the end of A & P rails via Chino Valley, Simms' Camp, Williams, and Flagstaff. THERE ARE NO INDIANS on this route. A THROUGH TICKET from PRESCOTT to NEW YORK is only $90.00. G. W. Ingalls, agent.

On the same page was a notice that Gilbert and Sullivan's *H. M. S. Pinafore* would play next week at the Prescott theater.

Christine laid the paper aside and at twelve o'clock went down to the dining room. A Mexican waitress gave her a small table by the wall. A long table down the center of the room was filling up with men — regular boarders who seemed to be businessmen and clerks from the plaza stores.

She listened to their talk, which was mainly about the westward progress of the railroad construction and speculation as to whether a branch line would be built to Prescott. She heard nothing about the voluntary surrender or arrest of Ron Garroway. A sensation like that would surely make a topic for discussion. "Didja hear about Frank Maxwell?" a man asked. "Got whacked over the head by a footpad up at Simms' Camp." "He'll be okay," another man put in. "Mother Monica stayed over a day to look after him. Her and Steve Mulgrave. They'll be in on the next coach."

Christine went back to her room, where a front window gave a full view of the plaza. Most of the buildings were shabby, but a few new two-story brick stores stood out. The cupolaed courthouse in the plaza park might have been found in the public square of any rural Midwestern county seat. Its basement had barred windows. The jail, Christine thought, would be in the basement. Was Ron in a cell there? Or was he hiding in some rooming house, fearful at the last moment to go through with his resolution to surrender?

Presently she saw a gang of prisoners come out of the courthouse basement. They were herded by a shotgun deputy. Three of them wore leg irons. These would be the more desperate, perhaps waiting trial for murder. Yesterday this same crew had watered trees on the plaza lawn. Was Ron now one of them?

With relief she saw that he wasn't. But it didn't prove he wasn't in a cell. Restless, she put on a coat and went down to the Gurley Street walk. She began circling the plaza, partly to see the town, partly to while away the two hours before stage time. She walked south along Cortez, then west along Goodwin, and in this block she saw the name Chad Granby. It was on an upstairs office window. Below it a window sign announced that here were the Prescott offices of the Skyline Mining Company, Chad Granby, President.

According to the paper the Skyline was a rich producer. On the same ridge where nine years ago her own father had staked a claim.

The prisoner brigade had today been given push brooms, shovels, trash sacks, and wheelbarrows. They were now sweeping trash and broken bottles from in front of the saloons, and cleaning away droppings at the hitchrails.

As they circled the plaza, Christine kept well ahead of them. From Goodwin she turned north along Montezuma, staying on the courthouse side of the street. The other side was an almost solid row of saloons and vice houses.

At the Gurley corner she turned east toward her hotel. A building or two short of it she came to Bashford's big general store. Its windows displayed clothing, hardware, groceries. One of the items was a garment Christine had felt the need of since arriving in this mountain climate: a short woolen jacket.

When she went in and tried it on, the jacket was a perfect fit. As she paid for it, she saw some fluffy yellow bath towels on a counter. She bought a pair, since towels furnished by the Williams House were not at all what she was used to. The clerk put the jacket in a neat box and made a paper package of the towels.

Christine took them to her hotel room. After unwrapping the towels she noticed that the wrapping was an old newspaper. A three-month-old copy of the *Miner*.

Would there be anything in it about the Skyline mine? With time on her hands, she skimmed through the news columns. The date of the issue was February 3, 1882. The only mention of the Skyline was:

Wages at the Skyline mine and smelter have been reduced from $3.50 to $3.00 per day. In protest, a number of men have quit and come to town.

An item on the same page reported:

The execution of John Berry for the murder of Mike Shores took place Friday. Berry was hanged in the Prescott courtyard before a large crowd of onlookers. Father Duraches led him by the hand to the gallows. They were followed by Sheriff Walker, Deputies Long, Herbert, and St. John. The scaffold timbers were the same as those used last fall for the execution of Crocker and Stallings.

Christine put the paper aside with a shiver. Would there be another item like that in a few months using the name Garroway? When next would they bring out those scaffold timbers to make a Roman holiday for the Prescott plaza? More and more Christine hoped that Ron wasn't in a basement cell over there. Yet where else could he be except hiding in some shabby room or running away through the woods?

The person to answer those questions was Steve Mulgrave, and just before three o'clock Christine went down to the front walk. A small crowd was gathered there. Exactly on time the stagecoach came rolling down Gurley Street, Steve Mulgrave on the box with the driver.

A chunky, short-legged ranch hand on the walk hailed him. "Hi, Steve! What kind of a price dija get for those steers?"

"Top money, Shorty," Steve told him. As he jumped down to the walk he asked, "Is the boss in town?"

"Yep, she's at her town house waitin' for yuh. We'd better shag over there right away."

Just then Steve saw Christine with an appealing summons in her eyes. He left Shorty and joined her at once. "Everything all right, Christine?"

She drew him aside. "With me, yes. But not with our friend Ron — I mean Arnold Andrews. He needs our help. Could you spare me a few minutes?"

Her earnestness made Steve go back to Shorty and hand him a check drawn to the order of the Kansas City Live Stock Commission Company. "Here's the steer money, Shorty. Take it to the boss and tell her I'll report later."

The stage passengers, including Mother Monica and Frank Maxwell, had by now disembarked. Maxwell had a bandaged head, but otherwise looked fit. He called a hack and put Mother Monica in it. "Take her to the Sisters of St. Joseph Hospital," he told the driver.

A few of the arrivals went into the Williams House; others dispersed toward homes or offices. Steve quickly rejoined Christine. "What's this about Andrews?"

There could be no privacy here or in the lobby. Christine looked across at a bench on the plaza lawn. "Could we go over there?"

Steve took her arm and guided her across the dust of Gurley Street. The bench was under one of the young cottonwoods which prisoners yesterday had watered by hand. Seated there Christine gave Steve a summary of what Ron Garroway had told her on the stage.

The ranch foreman listened gravely, then fixed his gaze on a crew of prisoners who now were sweeping up trash under the Bashford store hitchrail. He could see that the man he'd known as Andrews wasn't one of them. "Wait here a minute, Christine."

He left her and went to the courthouse, disappearing into the north basement entrance. Soon he was back again. "The cells are all empty," he reported. "Means our friend didn't give himself up. Which way was he heading when you last saw him?"

She pointed to the east side of the plaza. "I saw him walk past the bank and the Goldwater store with his bag. Looking for a room, I think."

"Mrs. Johnson's would be the first place he'd hit. I'll check with her."

Again Christine waited on the bench, watching the tall black-haired cowboy move with long, quick strides to the east sidewalk. The holstered gun still hung from his belt; she remembered he'd taken it from his satchel on the stage. Yet with the exception of law officers no one else on the plaza seemed to be armed. Then she recalled a printed notice on the lobby wall at the Williams House. It called attention to a town ordinance ordering all people entering Prescott wearing firearms to check them at a hotel or bar or livery stable within thirty minutes after arrival. They could reclaim them when ready to leave town.

For Steve the thirty minutes weren't up yet.

When five more of them had elapsed he came back with a report. "Our friend took a room at Mrs. Johnson's right after the stage got in. Shaved, changed, cleaned himself up, and left about a quarter to five. His belongings are still there."

"You think he changed his mind, Steve, about giving himself up?"

"Maybe. But if he made a run for it why didn't he take his stuff with him? No place to run except through the woods." Steve looked toward the wall of forest which sloped up from the south edge of town. "But he wouldn't make a run for it afoot. He's a saddle hand, so he'd do his running ahorseback. Tell you what. You go back to the hotel and wait for me. Just three livery stables here. I'll ask all three if anyone bought or rented a horse just after the stage got in yesterday. If our boy didn't do that, he's bound to be close by somewhere."

The first stable at which Steve inquired was the one where he kept his own horse and saddle. It was John Shull's barn at the northwest corner of Gurley and Montezuma. "Nope, Steve," the hostler said, "nobody bought or rented any horseflesh between four o'clock and nightfall."

Steve took off his gunbelt. "Better check this for me, Milt, before I get fined." A glance at the corral told him that his own roan saddle horse was there. So was Shorty Brill's sorrel. He didn't see Lem Hopper's mount. "Lem ride out to the ranch, did he?"

The hostler nodded. "Man named Conway came in on the stage yesterday. He'd seen your boss's ad about sellin' her place. So she sent Hopper out with him to show him around."

With Shorty and Lem, Steve made up the entire crew of Mrs. Emily Wardell's Half Diamond H cattle ranch. The three had driven her cattle to Holbrook, which a month ago had been the end of the A & P rails. While Steve went on to market with the beef, Shorty and Lem had ridden back to Prescott, leading Steve's roan and a trail mule. From now on there'd be nothing much to do except help the widow Wardell sell her land and ranch buildings.

Moving west on Gurley, Steve crossed Granite Creek and stopped at the O.K. Stables. The answer there was the same. No one had taken a horse yesterday after four o'clock.

It left only one other barn — the Antelope Stables at Granite and Carleton. Steve went there and asked his question. "No, señor," the Mexican attendant answered promptly. "I am sure no one takes out a horse at the time you say. And if he is a stranger, I would not forget. Only a spring wagon is rented from here yesterday, after four hours in *la tarde*."

It was hard to imagine Ron Garroway taking off in a spring wagon. Still it was possible. "Was it a good-looking young fella, well dressed, light-haired? A *gringo rubio*?"

"He is not like that, señor. This one I know very well. He has the name Ernesto, and I have seen him play pool at the Palace. He rents this spring wagon and pays in advance."

With a shrug Steve dismissed the matter from his mind. He knew by sight a barroom loafer and pool shark known as Ernie and couldn't imagine any connection between the man and Garroway. And since Garroway hadn't taken out a mount, he must be still in or near town.

Steve went back to the plaza and started down Whiskey Row. Eight saloons in this block, and all but two of them had wide-open gambling. The Plaza Bit, Daly's, the Exchange, Cobweb Hall, the Sazerac, the Palace, the Capital, the Nifty. Some had leg shows and dancing — although the real red-light houses were kept a block west of Granite Street.

Steve was right in front of the Exchange when a gunshot came from inside the bar. A constable ran up the walk and pushed through the swinging half-doors. An ordinary Whiskey Row brawl, Steve supposed. A mild curiosity made him follow the constable inside.

Bar customers were staring down at a man on the floor. He had a bleeding head and didn't move. Steve felt sure he was dead. His eyes went to a poker table. Three men sat at it with an empty chair at the table's fourth side. By his position the dead man had been sitting there.

One of the remaining players had a gun in his hand. He gave it to the constable with a shrug and a grimace. "He came at me with a knife; nothing else I could do."

The other two players confirmed it. The bartender spoke up. "That's right, Constable. The guy was losin' and he claimed Wilkie had a card up his sleeve. Pulled a knife and Wilkie plugged him."

Several of the bar customers gave the same version. Which meant that in court this would be adjudged a self-defense shooting.

Steve went no farther than the door — just far enough to see that the killer was his recent fellow passenger on a stage, Three-Card Wilkeson. This made the second time within a year that Wilkeson had killed a man on Whiskey Row. He'd gone scot-free from the other shooting and was sure to be acquitted again.

The ranch foreman hurried on to rejoin Christine. He'd just reached the Gurley corner when a sudden recollection brought him to a stop. In that other killing, some months ago, two key witnesses had saved Wilkeson. It had been past midnight at the Plaza Bit with only five men present: a sleepy night bartender, Wilkeson, the man killed by Wilkeson, and two other customers who swore that the victim had drawn first. Wilkeson, they said, had side-stepped the shot and then fired to save his own life.

Steve now remembered the names of those two witnesses: a sharp-faced little pool shark known as Ernie, and a bull-shouldered ex-barroom bouncer named Buck Sarg.

The same Ernie who a half-hour after the arrival of yesterday's stage had hired a spring wagon! A stage which had brought Wilkeson to town! Thinking back, Steve remembered Wilkeson looking askance at Garroway several times. Had he recognized Garroway?

If so, he hadn't gone to the courthouse to report Garroway to the law. It would have started a hue and cry, and there wasn't any. Was there a way to connect Wilkeson and Ernie with Garroway's disappearance?

Abruptly Steve turned back up Whiskey Row, and at the third saloon, the Palace, he went inside. The place had an ornate bar, glittering chandeliers, and lurid wall paintings. At the back was Prescott's best-equipped pool and billiard parlor. Steve went straight to the ball-racker.

"Has Ernie Jacks been in today?"

The ball-racker shook his head. "Not since four o'clock yesterday."

"Who was with him?"

"Some sucker he was trimmin'. Kinda funny, too, the way he hung up his cue and walked out; he let a cinch five bucks go down the drain."

"What do you mean funny?"

"Three-Card Wilkeson came in and said somethin' to him. Then he went out the front. Ernie hung up his cue and went out the back. Right in the middle of a long run."

"Did Wilkeson have a satchel in his hand?"

"Come to think of it, he did. Must've just got in on the stage."

"Thanks." Steve went out to the street, his brain churning with one probability and three certainties. The probability was that Wilkeson had recognized Garroway on the stage. The certainties were: on arrival he'd come directly here and spoken to Ernie; whereupon Ernie had gone directly to a stable and rented a spring wagon; after which Ron Garroway had disappeared.

Did it add up to an abduction? Steve hurried on toward the Williams House. At least he had a starting point — something to talk over with Christine.

CHAPTER
SIX

When another morning came, Christine was up early. She'd hardly been able to sleep at all, thinking about what Steve had told her yesterday. He'd offered a thin theory that Ron Garroway might have been picked up, knocked out, and hauled away in a spring wagon. It was all hazy in Steve's mind, nor could Christine herself make sense of it. What would anyone gain by it? The master mind, according to Steve's theory, was the gambler Wilkeson.

If there'd been an abduction, Wilkeson himself couldn't be the abductor. The entire town was talking about him right now; for late yesterday he'd shot a man dead in a barroom quarrel. This morning a coroner's jury would sit on the case. But the talk at supper last night was that a justifiable homicide verdict was certain, in which case Wilkeson wouldn't even be hailed into court.

Christine knew she wouldn't see Steve this morning because he'd be out with Shorty Brill trying to trace a spring wagon which a shady character named Ernie Jacks had driven out of a livery barn late day before yesterday.

Down in the lobby she bought today's *Miner*. Over her toast and coffee she read it and found no mention of Ron as either a fugitive or a victim of violence, nor any mention that he'd surrendered to the law.

Most of the current news was about gunplay at the Exchange Saloon. The loser in a card game had falsely accused the winner, then leaped at him with a knife, only to be knocked dead by a bullet.

Christine turned to an inner page. Mother Monica, she read, had returned from her tour of mercy along the A & P grading camps. Below this Christine read:

Frank Maxwell, leading Prescott attorney, is back from a trip to Kansas City. His many friends will be glad to know that he'll suffer no permanent injury from the blow given him by a footpad at Simms' Camp. Frank tells us he'll soon be making a ride out to the Skyline mine, whose legal affairs he has handled for several years.

Fred Williams came into the dining room and spoke to Christine. "A lady in the parlor to see you, Miss Mayberry."

The woman waiting for her in the hotel's small parlor was plump, sunburned, tightly laced, and seemed about fifty years old. She smiled cordially. "You're Steve Mulgrave's friend, aren't you? I'm Emily Wardell. Perhaps Steve mentioned me. He's my foreman, you know."

"Of course. He said you're in town now. I hope I didn't keep him too long yesterday. He intended to report to you as soon as he got off the stage . . ."

"He told me all about it," Mrs. Wardell cut in. "I think it's exciting, you and Steve trying to find out what happened to a friend you made on the stage. But that's not why I'm here, my dear."

She looked around at the parlor's shabby furnishing, then went on. "This is not a very suitable place for a girl to be staying, Miss Mayberry. Or may I call you Christine? I have a big town house, only a block from the plaza, where I stay when I'm not on the ranch. It has a comfortable spare bedroom . . . and . . . to tell the truth I've been awfully lonesome since Henry passed away. There's a cabin in the backyard, with bunks and a stove, where my riders bach whenever they're in town. Steve and Shorty stayed there last night. My other hand, Lem Hopper, took a prospective buyer out to show him the ranch — it's for sale, you know — but the main house seems awfully empty with just me alone. If you like, my dear, you could live there with me while you're . . . Steve tells me you came out to make some inquiries about a silver claim your father staked nine years ago, just before he disappeared."

Christine was at once grateful. "I'd be glad to stay at your house — as a paying guest, of course."

"Your company will be pay enough," Emily Wardell insisted. "Now suppose you go up and pack your bags while I call a hack."

At the same moment Steve Mulgrave and Shorty Brill sat their saddles in front of the Antelope Livery Stable. A Mexican barnman was pointing east up Carleton

65

Street. "I remember he drives that way in the spring wagon, señores."

"When he got to the next corner," Steve asked, "did you notice whether he turned into Montezuma Street or kept going straight ahead?"

"That I do not see. I am sorry."

The two Half Diamond H men rode a block east to Montezuma, then stopped. "He didn't turn to the left," Shorty was sure, "because that would take him right into the plaza." They'd already inquired around the plaza, and no one on any of its four sides had seen Ernie Jacks in a spring wagon late day before yesterday.

"So he either turned to the right here," Steve concluded, "or drove straight ahead up Carleton."

East on Carleton led nowhere, but the south extension of Montezuma Street was a well-traveled road up Granite Creek. So the riders turned to the right. For half a mile the street was lined with cabin residences. "You take one side, Shorty; I'll take the other."

During the next half-hour they covered the route for a mile south of town. Every answer was negative. Then Steve came to a house where a man was building a front yard fence.

"Hi, Rufe. Were you working on this fence late day before yesterday?"

"Yep; didn't knock off till nightfall. Why?"

"Did you see Ernie Jacks drive by in a spring wagon?"

Rufe was sure he hadn't. "I'd 've noticed him too. Because that loafer ain't the kind who drives wagons. Hangs around barrooms and pool halls allatime."

"Thanks." Steve rejoined Shorty Brill. "Let's go back and try Carleton Street.

They rode back to Carleton Street and turned east. The first block had a printer's shop, a blacksmith, and a few cottages. Inquiries at all of them brought no result. The next corner was Marina Street, and there Steve saw a woman hanging her wash on a line in the backyard. He stopped with his routine question.

"Ernie Jacks?" the woman said. "Don't know him. I was downtown shopping late day before yesterday. Didn't get home till after sundown."

"Thanks."

Steve was turning away when she remembered something. "Wait. I didn't see anyone driving it but I *did* see a spring wagon. It was just before dark when I looked out my kitchen window."

"Where?"

She pointed across Carleton Street to a shabby cottage of green clapboards. It had a deserted look and stood on the southeast corner of the intersection. "A spring wagon was in the backyard over there. No team was hitched to it. But there's a shed. Maybe the team was in the shed."

"Anybody live there?"

The woman shook her head. "It's been empty since March. Empty and for sale. When I saw the spring wagon I thought maybe someone had bought the place and moved in. But when I looked out next morning the spring wagon was gone."

Steve turned to Shorty Brill. "Looks like pay dirt, Shorty." They crossed to the empty cottage and dismounted. The backyard there showed wheel tracks. Narrow tires had gone in and out of the yard since the last rain. There was a ram-shackle shed, and in it they found sign that a team had been sheltered briefly there.

They went to the front door of the cottage and knocked. No answer. But the door wasn't locked. In fact the lock was broken, indicating that an intruder had forced his way in.

Steve looked in on a dusty, empty parlor with trash piled in a corner. A broken liquor bottle lay on the floor. A dark red spot on one of the floorboards looked to Steve like blood.

He saw a second spot farther from the door. "What do you make of it, Shorty?"

"I'd say someone got cracked down on, Steve. Maybe with a bottle; maybe with a gun. Could be your friend Garroway. Wonder how that guy Ernie suckered him in here."

"It's a safe bet," Steve concluded, "that Ernie wasn't by himself. Garroway's a pretty husky lad. Oughta take two to handle him."

"Unless Ernie gunned him," Shorty said. He looked for sign that a gun had been fired — an empty cartridge or a bullet hole in wall or ceiling.

"A shot would be heard in the street," Steve thought. "This looks like a conk on the head. Let's take a look in the other rooms."

A kitchen showed nothing. But in a bedroom they found a canvas cot with bloodstains at the head of it where a wounded man might have lain. The cot was the room's only furnishing. Steve shifted his gaze about, looking for anything which might identify the victim or his assailants.

It was Shorty who picked up what was left of a pair of steel-rimmed glasses. The lenses were smashed and the frame bent as though they'd been stepped on in a scuffle.

"That cinches it," Steve said. "They're Garroway's; he wore 'em on the stage. Can't figure out how they got him in here. But they sure as hell did; and then whanged down on him."

Shorty gave a low whistle. "They sure did. What for we don't know. Maybe they thought he had a wad of dough."

"They'd wait till after dark," Steve reasoned, "to haul him away from here. Couldn't risk it in daylight."

"Got any idea who'd be siding Ernie?"

"Ernie was hanging around with a bruiser named Buck Sarg one time when they alibied Wilkeson out of a murder charge. Which ties in. Sarg's a big guy with a strong back and a weak mind."

"If Garroway came straight here from Mrs. Johnson's," Shorty calculated, "he'd hit here about ten minutes before five. That's three hours before dark. So they must've held him here at least that long."

Steve agreed. For three hours or more the victim would have lain tied up and helpless on this cot. A close look showed two short pieces of stout cord, much like the pigging strings used on calves at a branding. One lay on the floor near the foot of the cot and could have been used to bind Ron's ankles. The other was near the head of the cot, on the right side, and could have been used to tie the prisoner's right hand to a leg of the cot.

It could mean that the victim's left hand had been free during the three or more hours he'd lain here. The left side of the cot was against a dusty plaster wall. Oddly shaped lines on that wall, just above the cot level, caught Steve's eye. "Looks like writing, Shorty. Two words. Can you make 'em out?"

The stocky cowboy gave a puzzled look and shook his head. "Don't make any sense to me, Steve. No reason to think our boy wrote it. What would he have to write with?"

"Maybe nothing but the finger of his left hand. That's a plenty awkward way to write when you're lyin' on your back. First letter looks like a G. Can't make out the next one."

"Could be an R written backward," Shorty thought.

"He'd lie there three hours listening to them talk," Steve reasoned. "They'd talk about where they aimed to take him. If he heard 'em name a place, he might write it on the wall with his finger.

The plaster was dusty enough to show the tracing of a finger. There were eight letters in all. As far as Steve could make out they were:

GЯOOM CЯK

After a study the answer jolted him. "If you turn the R's around it spells Groom Creek. That's it, Shorty. He heard 'em mention a hole-up on Groom Creek. So when it was getting dark — too dark for them to see what he was doing — he scrawled it on the wall."

The head of Groom Creek was only five miles south of here, and Steve had once picked up some Half Diamond H strays there. In the late sixties and early seventies there'd been some placer gold claims along Groom Creek, but they were mostly played out by now, leaving a scattering of deserted miners' cabins along the small, heavily wooded stream. It was a creek which generally went dry after mid-June.

"So what are we waitin' for?" Shorty said. "Let's go smoke 'em out."

Their mounts, standing outside, had saddle scabbards with carbines in them. "We might need side arms too," Steve decided. "I'll wait here while you fan down to Shull's livery barn and get the gunbelts we left there."

"I'm on my way," Shorty said. "Groom Creek, here we come."

CHAPTER
SEVEN

Shorty went out to his horse and Steve heard him lope off down Marina Street. He'd be back in a few minutes, and Steve spent the time looking for sign that could connect Wilkeson to the waylaying of Ron Garroway. He was sure Ernie hadn't been alone in it; the other man could be Buck Sarg or someone like him.

Steve looked in every room and again in the backyard shed. He found nothing except sign that a narrow-tired wagon had arrived and departed. Nothing to identify Ernie's companion. Nothing to suggest that he'd driven his prisoner to Groom Creek except two words scrawled awkwardly on a wall.

Thudding hooves announced Shorty's return. Steve joined him at the front gate, where Shorty handed him his cartridge belt with its holstered forty-five. A gun just like it rested on Shorty's thigh. "We're spoiling daylight, Steve. Let's ride."

They took the Montezuma Street trail south out of town and followed up Granite Creek for a couple of miles. By then they were in pine timber where an upgrade slowed them to a walk. "This sure nails the deadwood on Three-Card Wilkeson," Shorty crowed.

But Steve couldn't agree. "Not yet, Shorty. So far all we can prove against Wilkie is that he stopped at a billiard parlor and spoke to Ernie Jacks. He can claim Jacks owed him some money and he stopped by to dun him for it. He can say anything he wants, and we can't prove it's not true."

"He's in this up to his neck," Shorty insisted. "I'll bet my saddle on it."

They left Granite Creek and cut over a low piny ridge which let them down into the head of Groom Creek. The flow of water there wasn't bigger than a man's leg. "We can ask Old Man Hooper," Steve suggested, "if he heard a wagon go by late that night." Most of the Groom Creek claims had been abandoned, but a pioneer miner named Hooper was still at it, baching in his cabin and stubbornly reworking old gravel.

They hit the Groom Creek trail only half a mile above Hooper's place. The old man was stoking his pipe on the front stoop of his shanty when they drew up there.

"I turned in early," he said to Steve's question. "Some time before midnight wheel sounds woke me up. Can't say what kind of a rig it was. They's a party of hunters camped downcrik; thought maybe it was one of them."

"Thanks." Steve and Shorty rode on and found the next cabin along Groom Creek empty. Feathers and bones near it marked a spot where a fox or wolf had devoured a young turkey.

Further on a windfall log across the trail forced a short detour, and on this Steve could see the fresh prints of narrow tires. "We're right on their tail, Shorty. The old Warbuckle cabin's next. Maybe we'd better sneak up on it."

He remembered that in the lush days of Groom Creek the prospector Warbuckle had built his cabin a hundred yards back from the trail where a spring seeped from a shaly cliff. The riders reined away from the creek into tall ponderosa pine, alert for the sight or sound of picketed horses. "No shed at that cabin, as I recollect," Shorty said. "If they're there the spring wagon team oughta be in plain sight."

"It's a team of bays, the liveryman said. Keep your eyes peeled for them."

They heard a horse before they saw it. It was the chomping sound of a restless animal picketed in the sparse woods grass, impatient for better feed. A minute later Steve saw both the bays grazing at long rope, and some fifty yards beyond them he made out the log wall of a cabin.

For a moment the riders held their breaths, lest the picketed horses neigh at the approach of other mounts. It didn't happen this time. "We'll slip up afoot," Steve said as he dismounted.

"And get set to toss lead," Shorty added grimly. "Those jaspers ain't gonna like it, us walkin' in on 'em."

They left their saddled mounts, reins hanging, with the bay team. After taking the carbines from the scabbards, they advanced toward the cabin. On a footing of grass and pine needles their boots made no sound. The cabin's door was on the west side and closed. The north side had a window whose pane had been smashed out by hailstones.

At a nod from Steve they moved in a crouch toward the cabin's window side. When they were ten yards away they could hear voices. The first was a bull-throated voice which wasn't Ernie's. "We're givin' you one more chance, Garroway. Where'd yuh hide that money?"

Some inaudible protest came from a man almost too weak to whisper.

By then Steve and Shorty were at the window, crouching under it. The next voice was Ernie Jacks's. "He must think we're dumb, Buck. Expectin' us to believe the only reason he came back was to give himself up! He'd be beggin' for a noose. Wild horses couldn't pull him back here unless it was to dig up that dough. Tell us where it is, fella, and we'll let you go."

Again the answer was a tortured whisper.

Then Ernie Jacks again. "He needs more coaxin', Buck. Better give his arm another twist."

The cry of pain which followed made it impossible to wait any longer. It would be a close-quarters fight, so Steve and Shorty leaned their saddle guns against the cabin wall. They drew holster guns and slipped silently around to the front door.

"You take Buck, Shorty. I'll take Jacks." Steve kicked the door open and jumped inside with Shorty at his heels.

Ron Garroway sat on a wooden box, his face swollen with bruises. His left arm hung twisted. Buck Sarg stood at his left, and just behind him was Ernie Jacks. The big beefy-faced Sarg was gunslung. Jacks had no visible firearm, but a short-barreled shotgun lay on a nearby table.

"It's all over," Steve announced. "Up high with 'em, both of you. Sorry we didn't get here sooner, Garroway."

Jacks blinked at them, then jerked his hands shoulder high.

Sarg didn't. His knees bent a little as his right hand inched toward the butt of his gun. Shorty covered him, leaving Jacks to Steve.

"Please don't disappoint me, Sarg," Shorty begged. "Go for your gun. Biggest favor you could do me. Let's you and me shoot it out right now."

Sarg went for his gun, shooting from his hip, the move so lightening fast that his shot beat Shorty's by half a breath. His knees kept bending and he went down with Shorty's bullet in his head. His own had been quicker but less accurate. How badly Shorty himself was hit Steve couldn't tell. There was blood on Shorty's neck as he caught the edge of the door to keep erect. All Steve had time or eyes for was Jacks, who during the gunplay between Shorty and Sarg had snatched up the shotgun. He was pointing it not at Steve but at the back of Ron's head.

"You can down me," he admitted to Steve, "but not before I blow a hole through Garroway." His thumb

cocked the shotgun's trigger. "Make up your mind."
The little man backed slowly toward a rear door.

He can't get far, Steve thought. A cocked shotgun
could go off under the convulsive squeeze of a trigger,
no matter how fast Steve got his own shot off. The
important thing was to save Ron and get him to a
doctor.

What he didn't know was that Shorty Brill, right
back of him, was too dizzy from a bullet-creased neck
to be of much help during the next half-minute.

Keeping his shotgun aimed at Ron, Ernie got to the
back door. Nimbly he jerked it open and dodged
through it. "Stop him, Shorty," Steve said, "while I take
a look at Garroway. How bad did they beat you up,
fella?"

Ron's chin was on his chest and he didn't answer.
Steve looked at his dangling arm long enough to be
sure it was broken above the elbow. He heard the roar
of a six-gun outside and knew it was Shorty shooting at
Jacks. There was no answering boom of a shotgun.

A quick look told him that Sarg was dead. More than
likely Jacks was too, by now, so he gave his full attention
to Garroway.

"We'll haul you in to Mother Monica," he promised,
"and call a doctor. You'll need plenty of patching up.
Then we'll have to let the law in on it. Anything you
want to tell me first?"

"I didn't do it," Ron murmured.

"You told Christine you didn't do it. You came back
to give yourself up. Christine told me all about it."

A half-filled pint of whiskey on a shelf had no doubt been brought along by Sarg and Jacks. When Steve held it to Ron's lips, the bruised man revived a little. "We heard them talk, Ron. They couldn't believe you came back to Prescott for any reason but to dig up money. But who tipped them off? Was it Wilkeson?"

"They called him Monte."

Steve didn't know anyone named Monte.

Shorty came in with a bloody neck and a defeated look on his face. "He got away, blast him! And on your roan, Steve. Too many pine trees out back. Time I got there he was duckin' away among 'em. My neck stung like hell and it spoiled my aim. Him dodgin' from tree to tree — me chasin' him and too dizzy to shoot straight. Next I knew he hopped your roan and made off upmountain. Came back to pick up my saddle so I can trail him."

Steve made a fast decision. "Let him ride, Shorty. A county posse'll catch up with him. Right now I've got to haul Garroway to a doctor. First I'd better wrap up that neck of yours."

The cabin had a cot with a thin, frayed mattress, a small wood stove, and a bench with a bucket of spring water. Either Sarg or Jacks might have used it occasionally for a hideout. Steve bathed a scratch at Shorty's neck and wrapped a strip of cloth around it. "It burned like the dickens right at first," Shorty said. "Kept me from shootin' straight."

"You shot straight enough at Sarg." Steve nodded toward the man on the floor. "Now suppose you go hitch up the spring wagon while I see what I can find out from Garroway."

When the cowboy went out, Steve got Ron to the cot and put him on his back there. "Don't strain yourself, partner. Christine believes you and so do I. When you feel up to it, tell me what steered you to that Marina Street deadfall."

"Wanted to see a bartender," Ron murmured. "Night bartender named Wally."

"Why? Who tipped you to Wally?"

"Wilkeson."

"Where?"

"Banghart's."

Steve knew that Banghart's was the last relay station on the stage route coming into Prescott. "What spiel did Wilkeson give you at Banghart's?"

Pain from a broken arm kept Ron from answering. Steve opened his shirt and saw body bruises. This man had not only been beaten about the head but had been kicked brutally in the ribs.

"Take your time, Ron. Shorty and I are on your side. So's Christine."

There was nothing Steve could do about the broken arm except make a sling for it so that it wouldn't be jolted more than necessary on a bumpy ride to town. By the time he finished this, Shorty had the spring wagon at the cabin door.

"I'll take him straight to the hospital," Steve said, "then call in Doctor Day. After that I'll go to the sheriff and get him to send a couple of deputies and the coroner out. You'll have to sit on the evidence till they get here."

Shorty grumbled about it. His dizziness was over and he wanted to be chasing Jacks. "Come a big rainstorm and we'll lose him."

"That'd be better than losing Garroway," Steve argued. With Shorty's help he picked up the mattress, with Garroway on it, and put it in the bed of the spring wagon. The bruised man lay on his back, looking up at the sky.

Steve took the reins. "One more question before we start. Did those fellas mention Wilkeson by name?"

Ron shook his head. "They said Monte; only name they used."

"Most folks call him Three-Card Wilkeson," Shorty remembered. "That must be it, Steve. He used to deal three-card monte at the Plaza Bit Saloon. That's where he got the name Three-Card. But Monte would do just as well, wouldn't it?"

Steve nodded shrewdly. "It would do, all right. But proving it's something else. Go in and help yourself to a swallow of that whiskey, Shorty. Giddap." He flapped the reins and drove north toward town.

He took the long way because it was smoother going, and for a while he didn't bother his charge with questions. It was Ron who volunteered more information. "This Wally Merton bartender; it was just a name he made up."

"A name Wilkeson made up? Just what did he say?"

By fits and starts during the next mile Ron managed to relay what Wilkeson had told him at the Banghart station.

When the full story came out, it was clear to Steve why Ron had gone directly to the green clapboard cottage after coming out of Mrs. Johnson's rooming house. "You wanted to give yourself up. But it would help if you could prove you weren't the only one who'd breasted a bar with Crocker and Stallings a year ago."

"What will they do to me, Steve?"

"Depends on how good a lawyer you get. Want me to dig up one for you? What about Frank Maxwell? You met him on the stage."

There was a brooding silence before Ron answered, "Not Maxwell. Anyone else will do, but not Maxwell."

The ranch foreman turned and looked in surprise at the bruised man lying face-up in the wagon bed. "He's supposed to be the best in town. What've you got against him?"

"He lied about St. Louis." Ron closed his eyes and it was the last word he spoke on the road to town.

CHAPTER
EIGHT

The Sisters of St. Joseph Hospital was in West Prescott, on McCormick Street just off Gurley. An elderly handyman was sweeping off the walk when Steve drove up and called to him. "Help me in with a patient."

His luck was that Doctor Warren Day, resident physician for the hospital, was making his daily rounds when Ron Garroway was carried in. One of the sisters helped Day put him to bed. Mother Monica appeared and at once recognized the young man she'd ridden with day before yesterday on a stage from End-of-Track.

"It's Mr. Andrews!" she exclaimed.

Steve didn't correct her until Doctor Day had made an examination. Then he drew Mother Monica aside into the hall. "His name's not Andrews," he confided. "But I think he's on the level. Came here to give himself up for a crime he's charged with but probably didn't commit. I'll have to report him to the sheriff. If you want the lowdown on it, you can ask Christine Mayberry, who came in on the coach with us."

Steve went out and drove his spring wagon across the Gurley Street bridge and on to the courthouse. He took off his gunbelt and left it in the wagon, then hitched the team to a courthouse rack and went in by a basement door to Sheriff Joe Walker's office.

The sheriff, a genial middle-aged man with a brown mustache, was at his desk with two of his four deputies who were standing by for orders. Walker looked up and waved a hand. "Have a good trip to market, Steve? Sit down and take a load off your boots."

"Is Mr. Oliver around?" Steve asked. Ferd Oliver was District Attorney of Yavapai County.

"Up in his office, I reckon. Why?"

"I've got a report he ought to listen in on. Don't want to have to make it twice. What about calling him down here?"

The sheriff cocked an eye. "Whatsamatter? Find a body or somethin'? Okay." He turned to Deputy St. John. "Run upstairs, Roy, and ask the D.A. if he's got time to come down here."

In a very few minutes a lean, bony-faced lawyer joined them. "Steve here's got somethin' on his mind, Ferd," Walker said. "Fire away, Steve."

"A year ago," Steve began, "a young fellow named Garroway came to town on the stage from Tucson. A seatmate on the stage — a guy he'd never seen before — happened to be a no-gooder named Crocker. Only one vacant room at the Williams House, so they took it together. Next day Garroway bought a horse and rode out scouting for land to file on; had a little money and figured to start himself a stock ranch. When he got back to the Williams House coupla days later he found Crocker eating supper with a stranger named Stallings. Not knowin' anyone else, Garroway joined 'em. He —"

"Hold on!" Sheriff Walker was alert now. "You mean the three men who stood up the bank? We hanged two of 'em. Other one, Garroway, got away —"

"Listen to the way Garroway tells it," Steve cut in. "He says he knew nothing about that robbery. He was off in the hills when it happened. Heard about it two days later when he picked up a Prescott paper in a little store on the Verde. It said Crocker and Stallings had named him as the third man. It said the town was mad and there was lynch talk. So he panicked and made off east into the Mogollons. Got to Colorado and took a ranch job under the name of Andrews . . . After a year he got tired of hiding and came back to Prescott to give himself up."

Walker and his deputies sat gaping. Ferd Oliver asked sharply, "You mean he's in town now?"

"He's in the hospital," Steve told them, "with Doctor Day working on him. Someone beat him up to within an inch of his life. He's all banged up with busted bones and bruises —"

"There's a murder warrant out for him," the sheriff broke in. "Roy, you better go over there and serve it right now."

"Just a minute," Steve protested. "You don't need to worry about him getting away. The shape he's in, he couldn't walk ten feet."

District Attorney Oliver fixed a quizzical gaze on Steve, then spoke to Walker. "Let's find out how he got here, Joe, and just what happened to him."

"He got here by stagecoach," Steve assured them, "of his own free will and to give himself up. A girl named

Mayberry and I sat with him on the stage and he told the girl all about it. She passed it on to me. We figure he told the truth. Trouble is he was recognized by Three-Card Wilkeson, who was on the same coach. At the Banghart stop, Wilkeson gave him a bum steer."

They listened incredulously as Steve went on, giving him everything he'd been told by Christine and by Ron himself. How Wilkeson, arriving in town, had gone straight to the Palace Billiard Parlor for a word with Ernie Jacks; how Jacks had dashed off to rent a spring wagon and drive it to an empty cottage; how Steve and Shorty this morning had traced the wagon there.

"Where we found this" — Steve showed them a pair of broken eyeglasses — "and a tip that they'd taken him to Groom Creek. So we burned leather to Groom Creek and found Jacks, along with Buck Sarg, beating hell out of Ron Garroway."

"What would they beat hell out of him for?" Oliver questioned.

"To make him tell where he'd hid twenty thousand dollars a year ago. They couldn't believe he'd come back for any other reason. They kicked his ribs and busted his arm. Shorty and I showed up just in time to save his life. Sarg went for his gun and Shorty had to use a bullet on him. Jacks jumped on my roan and got away. Shorty's out there waiting for you to send a posse and the coroner."

Steve had to tell it twice before Joe Walker could piece it together. Ferd Oliver said, "Let's call in Wilkeson and hear what he has to say. He's just been cleared from a shooting at the Exchange; coroner's jury called it self-defense. Now here he is in trouble again."

Walker spoke to Deputy St. John. "You'll likely find him playing cards somewhere on the Row. Get him over here, Roy." To Deputy Kim Long he added, "Round up Millard and Herbert. Herb's on jailor duty and Millard's patrolling the plaza. The three of you pick up a rig and Coroner Burckhardt. Make time to Groom Creek. Which cabin is it, Steve?"

"The old Warbuckle cabin."

St. John and Long hurried away, and Steve spent the next ten minutes filling in details of a story some of which was hearsay and some of which was proven fact.

Then Roy St. John came in with the swarthy, flashily dressed gambler known to Prescott as Three-Card Wilkeson. "What's the charge?" he demanded querulously. "I paid my fine, didn't I?"

Although he'd been cleared of the Exchange Saloon killing, Judge Carttier had fined him twenty-five dollars for breaking the ordinance which forbade anyone to wear a gun after he'd been in town thirty minutes. Right now the man's holster was gunless.

Oliver fixed a stern eye on him. "You had a talk with Ronald Garroway at Banghart's station. What did you say to him?"

The glibness of the answer gave a hint that it had been prepared in advance. "So he was Garroway, after all! He was traveling as Arnold Andrews. I asked him if he had any kin named Garroway. He said no. I said 'You sure look like him.' That was all."

86

The law officers and Steve exchanged glances. There was no way to prove that the man's assertion wasn't true.

Oliver went on, "When the stage got in you went to a billiard parlor and spoke to Ernie Jacks. What did you say to him?"

This time the response came with a sly smile. "Everybody on the Row knows I made a trip along the A & P construction camps to decide which of those camps would fold up and which would become permanent towns. Did it for Gus Huggins of the Exchange Saloon, who figures to move his bar and games to the main line soon as trains start runnin'. It's gonna miss Prescott sixty miles, they say. After a look I decided that Flagstaff and Williams would grow up and the other camps would fade out."

"What's that," Joe Walker asked, "got to do with Ernie Jacks?"

"Just before I left on the trip Jacks told me he figured on startin' a pool hall up on the main line. Asked me to pick him a spot. So when I got back I told him the best spot would be Flagstaff. Anything else you want to know?"

"So when you told Jacks that," Steve derided, "he ducked out the alley door and rented a spring wagon!"

"Did he?" Wilkeson's feigned surprise was perfect. "First I heard of it. What would he want with a spring wagon?"

"That's what we're asking *you*?" Ferd Oliver said dryly.

The gambler's look said, "Ask and be damned." His lips said nothing.

Other questions couldn't shake him. "That's all for now," Walker said wearily. "We'll be looking you up later."

When the man was gone Steve asked the others, "Did any of you ever hear him called Monte?"

They hadn't. "They call him Three-Card or Wilkie," Walker said. "He's an old hand at dealing three-card monte."

"I'll ask around the plaza," St. John offered, "and see if I can tie him to that name."

"Meantime," his boss brooded, "all we got is Wilkie's word against Garroway's."

"And Garroway's." Oliver reminded them, "is the word of a man accused of bank robbery and murder — long a fugitive from Yavapai County justice. You'll have to serve that warrant on him, Joe, and put him in jail as soon as Doctor Day releases him from the hospital."

The sheriff nodded. "Dig that warrant out of the files, Roy, and serve it right away."

"Just one other thing I wish you'd do," Steve pleaded. "Go talk to a girl named Christine Mayberry. Let her tell you this boy's story the way he told it to her. She believes it. And she's not the kind who'd take up with a bank-robbing killer."

"Where can I find her?" Walker asked.

"Over at the Williams House. She —"

St. John broke in with a correction. "You're wrong, Steve. She moved over to your boss's house this morning. About an hour ago I saw her in the county clerk's office. Mrs. Wardell was with her."

It was news to Steve. "They were here in the courthouse? What for?"

St. John shrugged. "You'll have to ask Web Connors." Connors was county clerk. "All I know is they were looking at a big county map on the wall."

Abruptly Steve left them and went up one flight to the main floor. Connors and a woman assistant were in a big high-ceilinged office where county records were kept. Connors looked up when Steve hailed him.

"Hello, Web. I hear my boss and a Miss Mayberry were in looking at your map."

"That's right, Steve." The county officer thumbed toward a wall map. "The young lady asked me to show her where Milk Creek is. And Blind Indian Creek. I said they're south of here in the Bradshaws and only a couple of miles apart, with a ridge in between. Pointed the place out on the map."

"What else did she want to know?"

"She asked me to look up what month and year the Skyline was filed on, and who filed it. The books show that filing, of course. The filing date was August of eighteen seventy-three; prospector named Isaac Pendleton made the filing."

"Chad Granby owns the mine now, doesn't he?"

Connors nodded. "Chad owned half of it right from the start. He grubstaked Pendleton back in seventy-three for a half interest in whatever strike Ike made. Three years later he bought Ike's half and Ike went east to take it easy."

"You told Miss Mayberry that? What else did she want to know?"

Web Connors came to the counter and rested his elbows there. His eyes narrowed and he spoke in a lowered voice. "She wanted to know something that's none of my business — or hers either, far as I can see."

"Yeh? What did she want to know?"

"Asked me which assayer Pendleton and Granby did business with back in the days when they started the Skyline. Right then's when I buttoned my lips. Told her I don't keep tabs on who uses what assayer; and if she wanted to know, she'd have to ask Chad Granby."

"And what did she say to that?"

"Nothing. But Emily Wardell spoke up. Lots of folks in this town are afraid of Chad Granby but Emily's not one of 'em. She said, 'Thanks, Web; we'll go over to his office and ask Chad right now.' "

Steve went out to the rack where he'd tied the spring wagon. He drove it to Shull's livery barn and checked his gunbelt there. "This rig," he told Shull, "belongs to the Antelope barn. Have one of your boys turn it in there."

"Where's that roan of yours, Steve?"

"Fella stole it from me and left me afoot. Read about it in tomorrow's paper."

With no time for more talk Steve hurried across the plaza, heading for the Wardell house a block beyond. As he passed Sol Levy's bank on Cortez Street, he saw a professional shingle at the foot of stairs leading to second floor offices.

Ricardo Gonzales
Attorney-at-Law

Christine wanted him to recommend a lawyer, and he'd had the same request from Ron, who desperately needed one now. Christine's need was less urgent. And now there was a hint that she might tangle with Chad Granby. Until this morning he had intended to recommend Frank Maxwell to both Christine and Ron. But Ron had bluntly turned down Maxwell. Something about St. Louis which Steve didn't understand.

Now he remembered that Maxwell was attorney for the Skyline mine. From questions Christine had asked the county clerk, she seemed to suspect a fraud against her father either by an assayer, a prospector, or a backer who'd grubstaked the prospector. So there could be a conflict of interest if Maxwell should represent both Christine and Chad Granby.

On an impulse Steve went up the stairs and into a law office at the front. Law books filled shelves on two walls, while windows looked out on the corner of Cortez and Gurley Streets. An olive-skinned young man was penning a brief. "How busy are you, Rick?" Steve asked him.

Gonzales smiled and waved to a client's chair. "Not busy enough to need a secretary, Estevan, as you can see." He had a natural charm along with jet black hair and a mustache to match. His father, Steve happened to know, was a distinguished judge at Tucson. "You have stolen a horse, my friend, and wish to engage me for the defense?"

"Just the opposite," Steve said. "The horse was stolen from me. But I don't need a lawyer. Two of my friends do. They asked me to dig up an *abogado* for them. What about taking them on? It's two separate cases, you understand."

"New cases are welcome, Estevan. The answer is *si, con gusto.*"

"One's a gal and one's a boy," Steve said. "Let's take the girl's case first."

"*Listo.*" Ricardo Gonzales poised a pencil over pad, ready to take notes.

"Her name is Christine Mayberry. Her father came here nine years ago, found a rich silver claim, and then disappeared." Steve went on to relay what Christine had told him on the stage. Then he outlined the questions she'd asked at the county clerk's office today. "She's staying at Mrs. Wardell's house on Marina Street. Mrs. Wardell took her to Web Connor's office to look up a filing date. She found that the Skyline was filed only a few days after her father made a rich strike on that same ridge. Filed by a prospector who'd been grubstaked by Chad Granby. Just what do you know about Granby, Rick?"

The lawyer's dark Latin eyes narrowed shrewdly. "Only this, my friend. In the early days he was the town's money-lender. That was before we had a bank at Prescott. When a businessman needed money he borrowed it at a high interest rate from Chad Granby, and gave back a mortagage. The old-timers have told me that in the middle seventies half the stores on the plaza were in hock to Señor Granby. When debtors failed to pay on time he foreclosed, then sold the property at auction to get his loan back. Many who were treated that way hated him, and there were threats on his life. That is why he hires a bodyguard even to this day."

"You mean that Nevada gunman, Alf Sligo?"

"The same. For many years Señor Granby has never appeared on the street, or driven out to his mine and smelter, without Sligo at his side."

"What burns me up," the ranch foreman put in, "is that Sligo always packs a gun, in town or out. Rest of us have to check ours at a barn before we've been in town thirty minutes."

"That," Gonzales explained, "is because Señor Granby has great political influence in this county. He is the biggest taxpayer, so he persuades them to appoint Alf Sligo a special deputy. They say it is to guard bullion shipments coming in from the Skyline smelter. But we observe that Sligo never guards anything except the person of his employer."

"Let's get back to Christine Mayberry, Rick. According to cards in an eighteen seventy-three newspaper, the town had three assayers then. Adam Mayberry left his sample with one of them. Christine asked Connors which one was patronized by Pendleton and Granby. Connors clammed up and told her she'd have to ask Granby."

"And did she?"

"Yes. Mrs. Wardell took her right over to Granby's office."

Gonzales mulled it over, thinking out loud. "If Isaac Pendleton jumped Mayberry's claim nine years ago, then filed on it jointly with his backer, Granby, we can be sure that Granby has covered every track." Suddenly the lawyer sat up straight, adding. "Every track but one."

"Yeh?" Steve prompted.

"Assay reports aren't recorded. So there'll be nothing in the courthouse to show what happened to the ore sample left by Mayberry with one of three assayers on a Saturday evening late in July, eighteen seventy-three. But mortgages *are* recorded. They're no good unless they're recorded. Remember what I told you, *amigo*: that half the shops on the plaza back in seventy-three had to borrow money from Granby. Always he took a mortgage. Do you see what I mean?"

"I'm beginning to. Keep shooting."

"So I will look at the mortgage records for eighteen seventy-three and see if one of them covers a loan from Granby to a Prescott assayer. If payment was overdue, it would put the assayer in Granby's power. He knows well how to use power, this Granby . . . But let us do no more guessing, Estevan. If one hour from now you will bring the *señorita* here, and if she consents to be my client, I will perhaps have information of inportance. Yes?"

CHAPTER
NINE

Sitting between his employer and her guest in the Marina Street house parlor, Steve told them first about Ron Garroway. "He had a rough go of it, but he's in good hands now. Doc Day and the sisters'll take care of him. Sheriff'll serve a warrant, but the doc won't let 'em move him for a few days. Meantime I've lined up a lawyer for him. Ricardo Gonzales. He's workin' on your case too, Christine. Wants me to take you over to his office."

"Never mind my troubles, please. They can wait. Ron's can't." Christine said. "Will they let me in if I go to see him?"

"Tomorrow, maybe. Not today. Don't you fret too much about him, Christine."

"You sent the lawyer over to see him, of course?"

"He's looking up that assayer question of yours first," Steve evaded. "Fact is I haven't told him about Ron's problem yet."

The girl didn't like it. "Then let's tell him right away. He must forget my case until he's done everything possible for Ron."

After putting on her jacket and bonnet, she hurried Steve out of the house. A steep block down Gurley

Street took them to the bank corner. They could see the clock on the courthouse cupola. "The hour's up," Steve said as they took the narrow stairs to Gonzales's office.

The lawyer had just returned from the courthouse and was waiting. "I shall be happy to serve you," he said when Steve presented Christine. "Some things Estevan has told me; what he fails to tell is that you are so young and beautiful."

"He also failed to tell you," Christine said, "that our friend Ron Garroway needs a lawyer much more than I do."

Immediately Gonzales was serious. "He spoke of another case; one which has no connection with yours."

"We'll let you in on it," Steve said, "soon as you tell us what you found out about an eighteen seventy-three assayer."

"It will take only a minute," the lawyer promised. "I have looked at the book of mortgages recorded that year. One of them secured a loan of eight thousand dollars made by Chadwick Granby to a Prescott assayer named Harley Rood. The security pledged was Mr. Rood's house, shop, equipment, and personal property."

"Rood," Christine remembered, "was one of three assayers who advertised in the Prescott paper of that year."

"The county records also show," Gonzales informed them, "that in August of eighteen seventy-three the mortgage was lifted, and the lien on the property released."

"Which proves what?" Steve queried.

"It proves nothing, Estevan *amigo*, but it hints at much. The dates are interesting. Your father, Miss Mayberry, brings in a rich ore sample on the last day of July and leaves it with one of three assayers. He then disappears. A few days later a debt-ridden assayer becomes no longer in debt. Soon after that his recent creditor, Chad Granby, becomes half-owner of a rich mining claim located on the very ridge where your father made his strike. No one is ever able to find the stakes which your father must have driven at the four corners of his claim. No report was ever made on the ore sample which your father left with an assayer. Which breeds a suspicion; suspicion of a conspiracy among three people — a dishonest assayer, a greedy moneylender, and a grubstaked prospector named Pendleton. But alas, many years have passed during which all tracks may be well covered."

"What happened to Harley Rood?" Steve asked.

"The courthouse records do not tell us that. But I have just asked Fred Williams of the hotel. In eighteen seventy-three Fred ran a saloon on the plaza and was mayor of Prescott. He tells me that in September of that year Harley Rood sold his property here and moved to Wickenburg, eighty miles to the south. He is now the leading assayer there."

"And now," Christine broke in impatiently, "let's talk about Ron Garroway. Tell him about Ron, Steve."

First Steve made her repeat what Ron had told her on the stage. Then he took up the tale himself. "Three-Card Wilkeson was on the stage and recognized Garroway. He was dead sure that Garroway wouldn't

97

risk coming back to Prescott unless it was to dig up twenty thousand dollars. So he steered Ron into a trap. Couple of jiggers named Jacks and Sarg grabbed Ron and took him to a hide-out."

Steve quickly gave the rest of it. "So now Sarg's dead, Jacks is scootin' through the woods with a posse on his tail, and Ron's in the hospital all bunged up — with a murder charge hanging over him. He needs a lawyer and you're it, Ricardo."

Gonzales asked shrewd questions until he had every fact and detail involving Ron Garroway. "I shall call on him at once," he promised, "If it is his pleasure, I shall represent him in court. Until then there is only one real way by which we can help him."

"What can we do?" Christine asked.

"We begin," Ricardo said, "by assuming his innocence. In which case someone else was the third man who helped Crocker and Stallings kill a teller in a bank below this very office. I myself was sitting at this desk and heard the shots, I ran to my front window and saw three masked men riding fast away. If we can apprehend the third man, then there will no longer be a case against Garroway."

That, to Christine, seemed hopeless. "But the real third man by now may be a thousand miles away. After a whole year how could we ever find him?"

For a while Gonzales sat in deep thought, fingers drumming on the desk. "Let us consider horses," he suggested. "Two of the robbers were captured. The mounts they rode had brands — the brand of a horse ranch on Lynx Creek. That did not surprise or incriminate anyone, because the owner of the horse ranch only a day before the robbery had reported to the sheriff that three horses were missing from his pasture, which is a bare five miles from town. Strayed or stolen, he said. Would the sheriff please look out for them? Two of the horses were recovered with the capture of two bank robbers. It was assumed that the third robber rode the third horse far away to safety."

Steve's eyes narrowed as he caught the drift. "I get you, Rick. Maybe he *didn't* ride it far away. Maybe he just circled back to town and tied his horse at a plaza hitchrail. He could go into a bar and join the talk about what happened at the bank. Everybody knew him. No one would think that a horse tied outside was anything but what it looked like — the mount of a rancher just in from Lynx Creek. That Lynx Creek layout belongs to Cass Pomeroy."

The lawyer nodded. "How well do you know him, Steve?"

"Only to say hello. He doesn't run any cattle — only a small horse bunch which he handles himself. Sells 'em to Fort Whipple for cavalry remounts."

"This is my thought," Gonzales confided. "Crocker came to town by stagecoach, so he had no horse. The same was true of Stallings. So the unknown third man had to furnish all three horses. He must have been well acquainted with Crocker and Stallings, for this affair was clearly planned in advance. Let us suppose that the man is Cass Pomeroy. He prepares by informing the sheriff that three horses have strayed, or have perhaps been stolen, from his pasture. Actually he has them hidden in a shed, grained and saddled, ready for a job of robbery. In the dark of night he rides one of them to town, leading the two others. Crocker and Stallings meet him at some town barn. They mask themselves, and when the bank opens they raid it, then ride fast into the forest, where they separate, each with a third of the loot. Two are caught and Pomeroy circles back to town."

"It's a better case," Christine agreed, "than the one the law has against Ron. But how could we ever prove it — after a year?"

"It will not be easy," Gonzales admitted. "But a way to begin, I think, is to find out where Crocker and Stallings came from. Where were they born and raised?"

"Crocker registered as C. Crocker," Steve said. "No one ever knew what the C stood for."

"When a man is hanged," the lawyer pointed out, "it makes news in the papers. People in far places read about it. Even drifters and murderers have people somewhere — mothers, fathers, brothers, sisters. I well remember the day last fall when I look from my office window and see them hang Crocker and Stallings in the courtyard."

"I wasn't in town that day," Steve said.

"In all such cases," Gonzales went on, "the executed man's next of kin may claim the body. No one ever came forward to claim Crocker's body. But the family of Stallings had a loyalty stronger than their shame. The sheriff received a letter from an old couple who live in San Bernardino, California. They were the very sad parents of Stallings and they asked that the body of their son be shipped to them for burial. And it was done."

"Which proves?" Steve queried.

"That Stallings came originally from San Bernardino. And since they knew each other well, possibly Crocker did too. So let us find out where Pomeroy came from. If he came from San Bernardino, it will strengthen our case against him and in the same degree weaken the case against Garroway."

Steve was dubious. "It would help, but not enough. What else can we do?"

"There are places in Prescott," the lawyer suggested, "where men play cards or throw dice for money. Miners and cowboys sometimes lose everything at games along Whiskey Row. When a man loses his money, or becomes deeply in debt to other gamblers, he grows desperate and takes risks. Let us ask if Cass Pomeroy was a dice or card loser in the days before the bank holdup. See what you can find out, Estevan. Ask men like Dan McCurdy, who runs honest games, and Job Vance, who runs crooked ones — and Wan Sung of Chinatown, who is the biggest gambler of them all. And wait. There is a new place called the Hassayampa Hangout at Granite and Gurley Streets. See if you can find Pomeroy at any of those spots. If he was what we call a compulsive gambler a year ago, he still is."

"I'll get busy on it right away, Rick."

"And now," the lawyer announced briskly, "I shall go to the hospital and interview my client."

"And I," Christine decided at once, "will go with you."

They went down to the sidewalk and separated, Steve heading east toward the Wardell house, Christine and Gonzales heading toward West Prescott.

Emily Wardell was waiting at her front gate as Steve approached. When he told her Gonzales's theory about the escaping bank robber she was impressed. "Rick's a smart lawyer," she said, "and Christine's a smart girl. With a pair like that working for him, we don't need to worry too much about Garroway."

"What about a smart cowhand like me?" Steve complained. "Don't I get some credit too?"

Emily Wardell looked past him at an approaching rider. He was a small-built man with a sandy face showing under the wide brim of a range hat. "It's Lem Hopper, Steve. Wonder where he left Mr. Conway."

"Conway turned us down," Hopper reported as he dismounted at the gate. "Likes the layout fine but thinks we're overpricin' it. Offered ten thousand less than we're askin'."

The ranch woman took it with a shrug. "Very well, Lem; let him look somewhere else. It's a good furnished house and corral-setup, with good grass and an A-one ditch right. If Conway won't take it at my figure, someone else will. Go get yourself washed up, Lem, and put on a clean shirt. I want all three of you boys in for supper tonight. Want you and Shorty to meet our house guest, Christine Mayberry. Steve's met her and she's already got him looking kinda dreamy —"

"You mean Shorty's back?" Steve broke in. "I left him out on Groom Creek."

"Got back half an hour ago, Steve. He's out in the backyard cabin shining his boots. And listen, one other thing: we've sold our livestock and there's nothing much for you boys to do except chaperon prospective buyers out to the ranch and show 'em around. Lem can take care of that. Which leaves you and Shorty, Steve, free to help the Mayberry girl and the Garroway boy and their lawyer in any way you can. Just forget about the ranch, Steve, for the next few days anyway. That goes for Shorty too. See what you can do for Christine and that young man she's worryin' her pretty head over."

Hopper, knowing nothing of these matters, asked questions. When the name Chad Granby came up, he broke in with news of his own.

"Listen. Riding in from Skull Valley with Conway just now, we passed Chad Granby goin' the other way. He was in a buckboard with that gunslinger bodyguard of his, headin' lickety-split down the Wickenburg stage road."

Mrs. Wardell could hardly believe it. "That's funny, Lem. When Christine and I called at his office, he was getting ready to leave for his mine. His lawyer, Frank Maxwell, was going along because they had to settle some injury claim. Seems a cave-in broke a miner's leg and he threatened to sue; so Chad and his lawyer were hustling out there with a compromise offer."

"Looks like he changed his mind," Steve said, "all of a sudden. Right after you and Christine asked him some embarrassing questions. Took off for Wickenburg, and I can think of two good reasons."

"Which are?" Emily prompted.

"Number one, maybe he wants to get where you can't ask him any more questions about an eighteen seventy-three assayer number two, the assayer now lives at Wickenburg. So maybe Chad wants to tip him off; maybe get him to take a long vacation in Mexico, or somewhere."

All of which made plenty to talk about at supper that night in Emily's lamp-lighted dining room. Emily was at one end of the table with Christine at the other. Between them were three hungry ranch hands helping themselves liberally to fried chicken and hot cornbread, each with his own story to tell. Shorty wanted to talk about Groom Creek and three county deputies who, along with a coroner, had relieved his watch out there. "Millard and Herbert are tryin' to track Ernie Jacks . . . I wanted to go along but the coroner said nix. Said I'd be needed at tomorrow's inquest . . ."

Emily stopped him. "Let's not talk about inquests over victuals, Shorty. Christine, how did you find young Garroway?"

"He's a mass of bruises and has a broken arm, but no broken ribs, thank heavens. The sheriff has served a warrant on him, but they'll let him stay in the hospital for a few days. He likes that nice lawyer you found for him, Steve. And so do I."

Emily tried to talk about Chad Granby's sudden trip to Wickenburg. But Steve, watching Christine, could see that she wasn't at present interested in Granby. Or anything else except an early vindication of Ron Garroway.

"Is there any way," Shorty wondered, "to pin some deadwood on Three-Card Wilkeson?"

"Not till we can find someone who knows him by the name of Monte," Steve said.

"What will you do tomorrow, Steve?" Christine asked.

"Tomorrow," he promised her, "I'll go to work on Cass Pomeroy."

Later, in the backyard bunk cabin, he tossed sleeplessly. Deep, even breathing from the other bunks meant that Lem and Shorty were fast asleep. Steve's own brain churned with the shadowy figures of Chad Granby, Alf Sligo, Three-Card Wilkeson, a grubstaked prospector named Pendleton, and an assayer named Harley Rood.

When he finally fell asleep it was to dream an ugly dream: he'd gone down to Wickenburg by stagecoach to question Rood, only to find him with his throat cut, Granby's man Sligo had gotten there first, forever sealing the lips of a witness who knew the secret of Adam Mayberry's disappearance.

Waking up with a start, Steve drank a cup of chokecherry wine, and it put him to sleep again. This time his dream was pleasant — up to a point. He'd just earned a large reward for capturing the murderer Sligo, and with it had purchased Emily Wardell's Skull Valley ranch. No longer a mere foreman, he was asking Christine Mayberry to settle down happily with him on the Half Diamond H. But she didn't even hear him; she was looking over his shoulder at Ron Garroway.

CHAPTER
TEN

Most of the Prescott saloons kept open day and night. But Dan McCurdy's orderly place was locked and quiet from midnight till ten in the morning. At exactly ten o'clock Steve entered McCurdy's and found Dan in an office back of the bar.

"What about a little confidential information, Dan?"

"About what, Steve?" The two knew and respected each other. McCurdy liked to hunt quail in the fall and had always been made welcome on the Half Diamond H. More than once Steve had put him up at the ranch bunkhouse. And generally, when Emily Wardell's crew rode in on a Saturday night, their first stop had been at McCurdy's.

"About a horse rancher named Cass Pomeroy," Steve confided. "Do you know where he does his poker playing, if any?"

"Not here," the saloonman answered. "But I've seen him around. Seen his horse tied in front of the Sazerac a few times. Why? Does he owe you some money?"

"Not that. Just trying to find out if he ever got cleaned in a dice or card game. And if he ever bucks the wheel or box games. Got any idea who knows about it?"

McCurdy mulled it over. "If you go asking along the Row you won't get very far. The big dealers don't tell tales on their customers."

"Then how could I find out, Dan?"

"You might ask Jimmie-Behind-the-Stove," McCurdy suggested. "Buy him a couple of beers and he'll tell you anything you want to know."

It didn't take Steve long to find Jimmie-Behind-the-Stove. For years he'd been a familiar figure around the Prescott plaza. He'd arrived in the early days as a derelict remittance man from England, well-educated, well-mannered, lazy. Generally he sat behind a saloon stove and waited for someone to buy him a drink. Not to become a nuisance at any one place, it was his habit to pick a different saloon every day. His remittance from England no longer came. For eating money he occasionally swept a barroom floor or ran an errand for some customer.

This morning Steve found him behind the stove at the Capital bar. "Join me in a beer, Jimmie? Let's take a table."

Except that he hadn't shaved for a week, there was nothing trampish about Jimmie-Behind-the-Stove. His threadbare clothes were clean. He had blond good looks, a cultivated dignity, kept his fingernails trimmed, and even wore a necktie. Always he managed to appear shabbily genteel. Over the second beer Steve asked him, "Ever hang out at the Sazerac, Jimmie?"

"I am always welcome there. It is a respectable tavern."

Steve nodded. "Honest games, everyone says. Faro, roulette, needle wheels; but no magnets. Everything on the up and up."

"You are wrong about roulette and needle wheels," Jimmie corrected. "Nothing but a tiger box, dice, and cards."

"Rancher I know plays there once in a while. Cass Pomeroy. Does he buck the tiger?"

"I have never seen him play faro," the Englishman answered after a moment's thought. "Only poker. And that only in a private game. He has three cronies who meet him there on Wednesday afternoons. Not a house game, just a private session of draw poker."

"Big stakes?"

"Quite the contrary." By his precise accent, Jimmie-Behind-the-Stove might have come straight out of Oxford. "A twenty-five-cent limit, I believe. I doubt if anyone of the four ever lost more than twenty dollars at a session. Promptly at midnight they break up and go home."

"Pomeroy never plays with anyone else?"

"Not lately. But two years ago he sat in a big game in a back room at the Nifty. A six-handed game, this one. There was one big jackpot."

"Yeh? How big a jackpot?"

"It must have been big because people talked about it for a month afterward. Cass Pomeroy had a straight flush and a mine owner from Bumblebee kept raising him. Cass raised back till chips were piled high on the table. On the last call Pomeroy signed a deed to his horse ranch and shoved it into the pot."

"And lost?"

"No. He won. He raked in the pot along with the ranch title. He tore the deed into small bits and came out to the barroom stove. I was sitting behind that stove and I remember his grin as he threw the pieces into the fire."

"That was two years ago?"

"About two years, I think."

It was all Steve could get out of him about Cass Pomeroy. As he left the saloon, he tried to assess the significance of it. *He won that time. But if he was reckless enough to bet his ranch once, he might do it again — and lose! And need to recoup by holding up a bank!*

It was sheer theory, unsupported by anything except that Crocker and Stallings had ridden horses bearing Pomeroy's brand. Horses which the man claimed had strayed or been stolen from his pasture.

Steve spent the rest of the day going from saloon to saloon looking in on the dice, card, and wheel games just on the chance that Pomeroy might be in one of them. He wasn't. Nor was his horse tied at any plaza hitchrail. It wasn't a Wednesday, so he wasn't due for his regular draw poker session with three cronies.

No use asking house men or dealers about Pomeroy. McCurdy was right. They wouldn't tell tales on a customer. If Cass Pomeroy had suffered a big gambling loss a year ago, just before the bank holdup, the winning proprietor wouldn't want to talk about it.

A bartender on the Row who didn't even know Pomeroy said as much to Steve. "Here's another angle,

Steve. Most of us pay gambling license fees to the town of Prescott. A few corner-cutters don't. They hide their gambling in a basement or upstairs. So they don't dare admit either winnings or losings."

When Steve finished the plaza bars, he covered the several cheap joints on Goodwin between Montezuma and Granite. Turning north on Granite, he called at the joss house run by Wan Sung — who wouldn't admit that Pomeroy or anyone else had ever played fan-tan there.

Which brought Steve to the new Hassayampa Hangout at Granite and Gurley. It had only been running a few months, and what he had heard about it wasn't good. Word was that it was a rendezvous for toughs from the construction camps along the A & P railroad grade. There'd been an editorial in the *Miner* lamenting an influx of that breed into Prescott. They'd come originally, the *Miner* said, from the cowtowns of Kansas and Colorado, where they'd held sway as gunmen bullies during the seventies. When town-taming marshals had finally driven them out, many of them had drifted to end-of-track camps in New Mexico and Arizona, where for a brief time they'd lived by the law of the gun and strong-arm until the camps, one by one, broke up. Then on to the nearest likely hunting ground, which happened to be Prescott, territorial capital of Arizona into which bullion flowed weekly from silver smelters and where muckers and ranch hands brought their pay on Saturday nights.

It was at the Hassayampa Hangout, according to the *Miner*, that these railroad camp ruffians had found a harbor. A convenient spot for them, with the Granite Street bagnios in the next block south and the plaza tills only a square away.

The old-timers kept clear of it, preferring their haunts along Whiskey Row. So it wasn't likely that Cass Pomeroy had ever been in there. Steve was about to pass the place when he heard shouts and shots and smashing glass from inside. A brawl of some kind was going on. Nothing unusual about that, so Steve took a few more steps up Gurley on his way back to the plaza.

Then he heard a shouting voice which he recognized. "Drop that bottle! And be quick about it. You're under arrest!" The voice was Mel Leonard's. Leonard was town marshal, a hard-hitting young officer who for more than a year had been able to handle the worst brawlers along Whiskey Row.

Silence followed his command for someone to drop a bottle. Then his voice came again. "Are you hurt bad, Roy?"

Could it be the county deputy, Roy St. John? Steve crossed Gurley Street to find out. When he pushed through the swinging half-doors of the Hassayampa Hangout he saw a sawdust floor with two men lying on it. There was a barful of customers, most of them unshaven backwash from the grading camps. About half of them were gunslung, which in itself violated a local ordinance. Two of the guns and several bottles lay on the floor. Two or three men had bloody heads, which presumably in the last few minutes had been struck by flying bottles or fists.

111

One of the downed men, Deputy Roy St. John, got groggily to his knees. "I'm all right, Mel," he said. "Thanks for coming in."

It was at once clear to Steve that St. John had tried to stop a barroom brawl and had been batted down with a bottle. The melee couldn't have lasted more than a minute or so before the town marshal had rushed in to put a stop to it. There was no way to tell who had started the fight or who had struck down St. John.

Leonard looked around at the newcomer. "Lend me a hand, Steve."

"Anything you say, Mel."

To the room in general Mel Leonard announced: "I'm collecting every gun in sight. Owners can redeem them at the courthouse by paying the prescribed fine. Now listen, you bums. I'd just as lief shoot holes through you as not; so do like I say." He cocked his gun and the click reached every ear in the room. "Bartender, give my friend Steve Mulgrave a basket or a sack. Steve, walk around the room and collect guns."

During a half-minute of heavy silence Steve looked around a circle of sullen faces and knew that all this crowd needed was a leader. Luckily they didn't have one. Then the bartender tossed him an ice sack. With it he started toward the nearest gunslung man. He was halfway there when someone at the rear of the room threw a bottle. The aim was bad and no one could tell whether it was thrown at Steve or at Leonard. Leonard squeezed his trigger, and the bottle-thrower's howl as he went down echoed the roar of the gun.

In the next two minutes Steve collected eleven guns. By then Roy St. John was on his feet and had picked up his own gun from the floor. His head showed a bleeding scalp gash. "Can you make it to Doc Day's office?" Leonard asked him.

"There and back," St. John answered with a grin. "Let's travel."

Steve and the two officers backed out, Leonard with a cocked forty-five in his right hand and a sackful of firearms slung over his left shoulder.

A blast of profanity followed them, but no bullets or bottles. "About all we could do," Leonard said when they got out to the Gurley Street walk. "Couldn't arrest all of 'em. Some were just bystanders. Rest of 'em can get their hardware back by payin' a stiff fine. Thanks for siding me, Steve."

They left St. John at Doctor Day's office; then Steve and Leonard crossed to the courthouse. The marshal dropped his sack of guns on Sheriff Joe Walker's desk. Walker stared glumly as he listened to the report.

"Gettin' worse every day," he muttered, "since they started that Gurley Street hangout. A pack of camp toughs, footpads . . . with a few cold killers mixed with 'em. And me shorthanded!"

Leonard went out to resume his patrol of the town, leaving Steve alone with Sheriff Walker. And the term "short-handed" gave Steve an idea. He barely heard Walker's lament as the sheriff went on: "Three of my deputies out chasin' Ernie Jacks, who got away on that roan of yours, Steve. Only one left is Roy St. John —

113

and him now with a cracked head! If it wasn't for Mel Leonard, this town'd be in one hell of a shape."

"What about making me a temporary special deputy?" Steve suggested.

Walker gaped at him. "But you're workin' for Emily Wardell!"

"She gave me a short leave to work on something else," Steve told him. "I could do it better if I had a badge on. All I ask is that you let me pick my first assignment. After that I'd do anything you say."

"Yeh?" The sheriff's stare narrowed. "Just what assignment have you got in mind?"

"I want a search warrant to look through a house on Lynx Creek."

"Whose house on Lynx Creek?"

"Cass Pomeroy's. He plays poker at the Sazerac every Wednesday from noon till midnight. That's when I'd do it. So he'll never know I was there."

"And just what," Walker asked, "would you be looking for?"

"Something in his house that would indicate he was raised at or near San Bernardino, California. Or anything that could tip us he ever knew Crocker or Stallings."

"Keep talking, Steve."

"When you caught up with Crocker and Stallings they were riding mounts with Pomeroy's brand on them. How do we know Pomeroy didn't furnish them? How do we know that Cass himself wasn't the third bank robber?"

114

Walker pursed his lips, thought a minute, then shook his head. "Two witnesses said the third man was Ronald Garroway."

"Outlaw witnesses," Steve reminded him. "Crocker and Stallings. They had nothing to lose by naming Garroway. And plenty to gain. Pomeroy could have circled back to town, big as life. Maybe he needed money and figured to get it by calling in two old pals to help him rob a bank."

"Why would he need money? He's got a first-class horse ranch, clear."

"A ranch he once bet on a poker hand. Ask Jimmie-Behind-the-Stove. He happened to win that particular pot. But if he'd take a risk like that once he'd take it again and maybe lose. By the way, Joe, who was defense lawyer at the trial of Crocker and Stallings?"

"Tom Rush, as I remember."

"Rush doesn't work for nothing. Who paid his fee?"

"Crocker did. The fee was five hundred cash."

"What did Crocker have on him when you picked him up?"

"Nothing but twenty thousand in bank loot and some pocket change."

"You took the pocket change and gave him a receipt for it. So where did he get the five hundred dollars to pay Rush?"

Walker gave a sheepish shrug. "We didn't search him good enough. He had five hundred dollars cached in the lining of his boot."

"That's what he'd tell you," Steve countered. "But suppose the third man was Pomeroy. Pomeroy who got

115

clean away with his own cut. He could slip up to a cell window any dark night and toss five hundred bucks through the bars. He'd be afraid not to. If he didn't, his partners could peach on him any time they wanted."

"You're guessing," Walker persisted.

"So are you and Oliver," Steve argued, "when you build your case against Garroway on the word of two outlaws and the fact that Crocker and Garroway happened to hit town on the same stage and take the only room Fred Williams had left."

"I've already served a warrant on Garroway. We'll leave him in the hospital a couple of days longer and then bring him to a county cell."

"That'd be Thursday. So what about letting me search Pomeroy's house Wednesday afternoon, with a legal warrant?"

Joe Walker gave a shrug of capitulation. "Okay, Steve. Short-handed like I am, I can't very well turn you down."

CHAPTER
ELEVEN

At a little after midday Wednesday Steve took a post at the north end of Whiskey Row from which he could see the Sazerac hitchrail. A saddle horse he'd rented from Shull was tied around the corner on Gurley. His gunbelt hung from the saddle horn, and the badge Walker had given him was out of sight in his pocket. He'd confided in no one, not even in Christine and Emily Wardell. No use getting their hopes up until he could back up his suspicion of Pomeroy with some solid evidence.

When he saw Cass Pomeroy ride up to the Sazerac hitchrail, he had to admit that the man didn't look like a bank-robbing killer. Right now he'd pass for any sober and substantial stockman. A square-cut man in a corduroy jacket, Stetson range hat, and denim pants, booted and spurred, about forty years old and clean-shaven, with a holstered forty-five at his hip which he'd be entitled to wear for the next thirty minutes. He could check the gun at Sazerac's bar and reclaim it when the game broke up at midnight.

Steve knew little about him except that he was unmarried and lived alone on Lynx Creek, where he needed no help in taking care of some fifty pastured horses. The mount he rode today was a strong black gelding. All the

Pomeroy horses were solid colors, since his main market was remounts for cavalry stationed at Fort Whipple. Cavalry specifications were tight — solid-color geldings, bays, or blacks, five to eight years old.

A few such mounts sold each season would bring enough to keep Pomeroy in groceries and tax money.

When the man went into the Sazerac, Steve waited ten minutes, then strolled past the place. Looking over the half-doors he could see Pomeroy, now gunless, sitting at a barroom card table. The three men with him, one of them already shuffling a deck, were known to Steve as citizens of good reputation. A Goodwin Street feed store man, a hay rancher from Chino Valley, and an off-duty stagecoach driver. Their solid respectability made Steve dubious — and glad that he hadn't confided his scheme to anyone but Joe Walker.

The Sazerac barman carried four mugs of beer to the poker table. By then the first hand had been dealt. It should mean a clear field till midnight for Steve. He went around the corner to his horse, mounted, and rode east out of town.

As he cleared the last house, Fort Whipple's barracks could be seen a short way off to the left while to his right loomed the timbered skyline of the Bradshaw Mountains. It was only five miles to Lynx Creek, which was a small tributary to the Agua Fria. A low piny ridge divided it from the Granite Creek watershed, and as soon as Steve was in the pines he buckled on his gunbelt and pinned the badge on his jacket.

The five miles took only an hour, and shortly after two o'clock he rode into Cass Pomeroy's barnyard. It

118

had the deserted look he'd expected. A little way off to the left a line of cottonwood and willow marked the course of Lynx Creek. A ditch from the creek ran through Pomeroy's corral, which was now empty of stock. The house had rock walls and a shingle roof, a downspout from the roof leading to a cement cistern. A pair of half-grown cottonwoods shaded the yard, and a few chickens were in sight. In a pasture beyond Steve saw grazing horses.

He dismounted at the barn, tied his mount, and walked quickly to the front door of the house. A search warrant was in the inner pocket of his coat, but it wasn't likely he'd need to show it. On the off-chance that someone might be inside, he rapped his knuckles on the door. No one answered. The window shades were down. Except for the distant grazing horses and a few hens, no life was in sight.

He tried the door and found it locked. He circled the house and tried the kitchen door. It too was locked. But ranch doors usually had cheap, standard locks. Steve brought out a bunch of five-cent keys and began trying them. One of them brought a click and he opened the kitchen door.

Inside he raised a shade to let in light. Then he lighted a kerosene lamp and began exploring. There were four rooms, unusually tidy for a bachelor's house. They were all square and plainly furnished — a kitchen, a bedroom, a sitting room, and a room with a swivel chair and desk where Pomeroy evidently kept his accounts. Only the sitting room had a carpet. The others had oilcloth floors. The bedroom and office had a few small throw rugs made from bear and wolf hides. The sitting room had a stone fireplace with a mantel over it.

Walls had no decorations except commercial calendars. But on the fireplace mantel was a framed photograph showing a woman of about Cass Pomeroy's age who looked enough like him to be a sister. Steve examined the photographer's label, hoping it would be San Bernardino, California. Instead it was Wichita, Kansas.

A desk in the office seemed the best place to begin. The desk drawers had numerous old letters, receipted bills, and a small ledger showing horse sales. Steve set his lighted lamp on the desk and began sorting through the old letters.

He found no San Bernardino postmarks, no California postmarks whatever. Most of the envelopes had been thrown away. Most of the ones he found had Arizona postmarks and enclosed letters of routine business. There were tax receipts and a sheriff's receipt for a fine Pomeroy had recently paid for wearing a gun longer than thirty minutes after arriving in town.

One of the old letters was in a woman's handwriting and was dated at Wichita, Kansas, about two years ago. It was signed, "Your loving sister, Ruth." This would be the woman whose photograph was on the mantel.

Steve read the letter for whatever hint it might give of Pomeroy's connections and past. A paragraph near the end impressed him and he read it twice.

. . . since Claude left me I've been teaching in the grade school here. The divorce was granted last month. With no one to look after but myself, I've sold the old house and moved into a nice little flat. I'd be happy if you'd surprise me with a visit some time.

It was the name "Claude" which made Steve read the letter twice. Or rather it was the fact that the name began with a C. For this sisterly letter was written on monogrammed stationery, suitable for a lady's notepaper. The monogram at the top of the sheet was an R superimposed over a C. The R clearly stood for Ruth.

Could the C stand for Crocker? Could the man who'd been divorced two years ago by Ruth have been Claude Crocker? Lots of names began with C. Steve remembered that Crocker, arriving on a stagecoach a year ago with Ron Garroway, had signed the Williams House register with the name "C. Crocker." He'd never admitted to any other name. He could have been Charles or Carl Crocker.

But if C stood for Claude, then there could be little doubt that Claude Crocker, hanged in the Prescott courtyard last fall, had been a brother-in-law of Cass Pomeroy. It would establish a solid connection between Pomeroy and Crocker.

Steve put Ruth's letter in the inside pocket of his jacket and went on with his search of the desk. Maybe he could find another letter to which the sister had signed her full married name. But there wasn't any, nor any mention of the name Crocker.

A bookstand in the room had a few dozen books. Steve looked through them for a name on a flyleaf. Some were very old and worn, perhaps dating from Pomeroy's life in Kansas. One of them was a textbook on American history with the name Ruth Pomeroy on the inside cover. She must have owned it before her marriage to Claude.

The bedroom closet had an overcoat, a sheepskin storm jacket, and two extra suits. They'd been sold by the C.P. Head store in Prescott. In their pockets Steve found nothing of interest. A shoebox full of odds and ends had the name of a Wichita, Kansas, bootery on it, which confirmed that Pomeroy had originally come from Wichita.

When he'd covered all four rooms, Steve left the house by the front door and went to the barn. The harness and saddle rooms had work garments hanging from pegs. Again the pockets offered nothing. A battered range hat had a haberdasher's name on the sweatband: a shop in Wichita, Kansas.

After half an hour at the barn, he went back to the house. Only the desk drawers had yielded anything of value, so he decided to go through them again. There were six drawers, three on each side. He took them one at a time, emptying everything out on the desk top.

The only thing he found which he'd overlooked before was a receipted bill for fifty dollars from a Prescott lawyer named Thomas Rush. It covered a ditch-right litigation two years ago for which Rush had represented Pomeroy in court.

The same Tom Rush a year ago had defended Crocker and Stallings. Was it a coincidence? Rush was a highly reputable attorney. But if Cass Pomeroy had tossed five hundred dollars through cell bars for a defense fee, might he not also have recommended an attorney? Crocker and Stallings were strangers in Prescott. In choosing a lawyer they'd need advice from someone who'd lived here a long time.

It was only a thin clue, but Steve put the receipted law bill in his pocket along with Ruth C.'s letter.

He was sliding the last drawer back into the desk when heard a sudden ominous click behind him. He was in an awkward position, on his knees in front of the desk. Twisting around he saw Cass Pomeroy in the doorway aiming a cocked forty-five at him.

The man looked mad, rather than guilty or scared. "I could kill you," he said, "for a house-breaking trespasser. What the hell do you think you're doing, Mulgrave?"

Steve raised his hands shoulder high and got slowly to his feet. It put him face to face with Pomeroy, who could now see the badge on his jacket. "I've got a search warrant," Steve said. "Want to see it?"

"A search warrant," Pomeroy snapped, "can't be used until it's been served. You didn't serve it. Which leaves you a plain sneak-thievin' snooper, and by rights I ought to blast a hole through you."

Steve had never looked up the law, but he had a feeling that the man was technically right. A search warrant had to be served before it could properly be used. He'd counted on Pomeroy staying at the Sazerac game until midnight.

Why hadn't he? Maybe some barroom gossip had tipped the man that Steve had spent a whole day inquiring about his gambling habits all along the Row. Or maybe the courthouse clerk who'd made out the search warrant had leaked the information which somehow had found its way to Pomeroy.

In any case here he was with a cocked gun and in a temper to use it. He was in his own house and had caught a forced-entry intruder in the act of searching his desk.

"All I came for," Steve said, "was to find out if you'd ever lived at San Bernardino, California." That much was literally true.

"Yeh?" Pomeroy challenged. "Keep talkin'."

"Stallings came from San Bernardino. So maybe you and Crocker did too. Seems I was wrong. Can't find anything which ties you to San Bernardino. Or Crocker either."

The man with the cocked gun seemed to relax a little. "What kind of a tree are you barking up, Mulgrave? What the hell would I have to do with those two hang-birds?"

"The horses they were on had your brand. You said they were stolen and maybe they were. But there was a bare chance you'd furnished them, so Gonzales wanted me to find out for sure."

"You mean Rick Gonzales, the Mex lawyer? What's he got to do with it?"

124

"He's defending Ron Garroway, who was tabbed as the third robber. The one that got away."

Pomeroy's gun was still cocked and aimed at Steve's head. His face was a poker player's mask. "Want to see the search warrant?" Steve asked again.

The man shook his head. "If you didn't have that badge on," he said coldly, "I'd blow you down."

If he did there'd be no penalty, Steve thought. The law would call it justifiable homicide — a householder having caught a break-in prowler rifling his desk. On the other hand, if Pomeroy was in fact the third bank robber, he'd want as little attention as possible drawn toward him. Letting the prowler ride away unharmed would help to put him in the light of a peaceable citizen incapable of robbing a bank and shooting a teller.

All this flashed through Steve's mind and made him decide not to mention the sister in Wichita or the monogram on her notepaper or an ex-husband named Claude. "Looks like I got caught off base," he said wryly.

It tipped the scales in favor of dismissal. "All right," Pomeroy said grudgingly. "Now get to hell outa here. Next snooper I catch breakin' into my house'll get a bellyful o' lead."

Keeping his hands shoulder high, Steve walked past him and out of the house. His saddled horse was tied in front of the barn. The animal would have been seen at a distance by Pomeroy, allowing him to slip up stealthily on the intruder.

★　★　★

Steve was halfway to town before it occurred to him that there was a quick, easy way to find out Ruth Pomeroy's married name. Fort Whipple was connected by a military telegraph wire to Fort Wingate, New Mexico, which in turn had a commerical telegraph connection with Albuquerque and points east.

So a telegram from Sheriff Walker to the sheriff at Wichita, Kansas, should promptly answer the question. What was the married name of a Wichita schoolteacher whose maiden name had been Ruth Pomeroy and who'd divorced a man named Claude?

If a telegram like that were filed tonight, there should be an answer by noon tomorrow.

At sundown Steve rode into the Prescott plaza and found Ricardo Gonzales still in his office over the bank. He showed the lawyer a letter signed "Your loving sister, Ruth."

Gonzales saw the name Claude and looked at the monogram RC. "You have done well, Estevan. Let us now go to the sheriff."

Joe Walker had closed his courthouse office for the day, but they found him at his home on Alarcon Street. He read the letter and listened gravely to Steve's story.

"C" he said, "could stand for Campbell or Cramer. If it does we've got nothing on Pomeroy. But if it stands for Crocker we'll get out a warrant for his arrest."

"If you'll write a telegram to Wichita," Steve offered, "I'll ride to Fort Whipple and file it."

Walker nodded. It was less than a mile to Fort Whipple, and twenty minutes later Steve had filed a telegram with the military operator there.

126

Then he rode to Emily Wardell's town house and found her at supper with Christine. "Keep your fingers crossed, everybody." Jubilantly he told them about the Wichita telegram. "An even chance that Ron won't see the inside of a jail. All it takes is a right answer from Wichita."

It was a night of suspense while they waited. Early in the morning Steve rode to the Fort Whipple telegraph office with Joe Walker. Nothing had come in yet. The sheriff stoked his pipe and Steve twisted a cigarette. "It's an hour later in Kansas," the operator said. "But the wires are slow. Not likely to get an answer before noon."

Walker paced the floor, his eye on the clock. Steve was hardly less impatient. "Look, Joe. Maybe he's remembered that letter from Ruth by now. It's missing from the desk, so he'll know I took it. He'll remember it mentions Claude. So if he's our man he'll get the wind up, won't he?"

"You mean he might make a run for it? Maybe. But he'd be more likely to stand pat and bluff it out. Anyway we'll know in an hour or so."

It was past noon when the answer came.

Sheriff J. Walker,
Prescott:
   Ruth Pomeroy local schoolteacher married Claude Crocker 1875 divorced same 1880.
                     Ramsey, Sheriff, Wichita

127

Walker gave it a look, then with a grim nod hurried to his horse. Steve followed and the two cut directly east at a gallop, bypassing Prescott. "I had a talk with Ferd Oliver last night," the sheriff said. "If C stands for Crocker, I'm to arrest Pomeroy and drop the charge against Garroway."

They pulled to a walk as the trail climbed toward a divide. Once over it they spurred to a canter and presently rode through Cass Pomeroy's gate.

Again the house had a deserted look. The barn and corral were empty. The saddle Pomeroy had used yesterday was missing from its rack.

Nor was there any sign of the black gelding saddle horse.

"He likely rode to town," Walker guessed. "Right now he'll be breasting a bar on the Row."

"Either that," Steve worried, "or he's flown the coop."

When they tried the front door, it wasn't even locked. They went in, and the first thing Steve saw was a dislodged stone on the fireplace hearth. A gaping square hole in the stone face of the fireplace told its own story, "That's where he kept it," Steve said glumly. "He'd be afraid to put it in a bank."

The sheriff nodded. He knew Steve meant a twenty-thousand-dollar cut of the bank loot. "He'd use five hundred of it to pay his pards' lawyer fee, and maybe some more of it to pay off a gambling debt. The rest he'd have to cache somewhere. Somewhere handy where he could light out with it on short notice."

Steve looked in the bedroom and saw that the bed hadn't been slept in. "So he's long gone in the hills by now. Must have left right after dark last night. He'd be smart enough to know we could wire Wichita and check up. Gives him a twenty-hour start."

The sheriff made a grimace. "Anyway," he concluded, "it blows up the case against your friend Garroway. Let's ride to town and tell Ferd Oliver."

"You tell Oliver," Steve said as he swung to his saddle. "I'll be busy telling Ron Garroway and a gal named Christine."

CHAPTER
TWELVE

Three days after the disappearance of Cass Pomeroy, Ricardo Gonzales held what he called a strategy meeting in his office over the bank. During those three days the law had searched in vain for both Pomeroy and Ernie Jacks. Ron Garroway during that time had been released from the hospital, and the year-old charge against him had been dropped by the County of Yavapai, Territory of Arizona.

Except that his left arm was in a sling, its bone set in splints, Ron seemed fully recovered from his rough treatment at the Groom Creek cabin. With him in Gonzales's office were Christine Mayberry and Steve Mulgrave.

"It is now time," the lawyer announced, "to begin the investigation of Chad Granby."

"Count me in on it," Steve said briskly.

"Me too," Ron chimed in. "After what you people did for me, I want to pitch in and help any way I can."

"Is it true," Christine asked, "that Mr. Granby has returned from Wickenburg?"

"He sure has," Steve confirmed. "Came back in a private conveyance with his bodyguard Sligo. Couldn't have stayed in Wickenburg more'n a night or two."

130

"Which convinces me," Gonzales concluded, "that he went down there merely to warn an assayer named Harley Rood that Adam Mayberry's daughter has turned up to ask questions about what happened nine years ago. So more than ever I suspect a conspiracy. It would be an eighteen seventy-three conspiracy involving an assayer, a moneylender, and a grubstaked prospector to defraud and perhaps to murder Adam Mayberry. Already I have learned one thing, *amigos*."

"Yes?" Christine prompted.

"We know that the Skyline mining claim was originally owned half-and-half by Granby and the prospector Pendleton. The claim was recorded under that joint ownership in August eighteen seventy-three. Granby furnished development money, and the mine became a bonanza. In eighteen seventy-five he built a small smelter on Milk Creek, a mile downhill from the ridgetop on which the claim is located, around which the settlement of Granby has grown up. The place now has several hundred people. The mine and smelter crews live there. Ore is carted down from the ridge and reduced at the Granby smelter, from which bullion bars come regularly to Prescott and from here are sent by stagecoach and rail to San Francisco. The mine has dumped a vast fortune into the lap of Chad Granby."

Ron asked, "What about Isaac Pendleton?"

"In eighteen seventy-six Pendleton sold his fifty-percent interest to Granby and moved east to enjoy a life of ease. I have looked in the county books to find the terms of this recorded sale, and find that Pendleton receives from Granby a lifetime annuity of one

131

thousand dollars per month. The annuity will terminate at Pendleton's death. I then went to Joshua Finch to confirm this fact."

"Who." Christine asked, "is Joshua Finch?"

"He is auditor and treasurer of the Skyline company, a friend of mine and an honest man. He tells me that a check for one thousand dollars has been sent to Pendleton each month for the last six years. Señor Finch has the cancelled checks on file. They were cashed at a bank in St. Louis, Missouri, where Pendleton now lives. It has been a good investment for Chad Granby, since the Skyline is now netting a hundred thousand dollars per year."

Steve gave a low whistle. "That's a pile of dough. And if Adam Mayberry's claim was jumped, by rights it belongs to Christine."

"We could file a suit in her behalf," Gonzales told them, "if we could prove a conspiracy among Granby, Pendleton, and the assayer Rood. All three should be watched and questioned. So I propose the following: that I go at once to St. Louis and question Pendleton — if guilty he will lie, but perhaps he is not a very good liar — that Steve goes to Milk Creek, and that our young friend Ron Garroway goes to Wickenburg. Steve can spend a few days at the smelter town of Granby, and on the ridge above it where Adam Mayberry filed the Newbern claim nine years ago, keeping his eyes and ears and mind open; and Ronald can go by stage to Wickenburg to learn what he can about Harley Rood."

The broad scope of the proposal amazed Christine. "But this," she protested, "would cost a great deal of money, and I have very little."

"I will take the case," Gonzales assured her, "on a contingent basis. My fee will be a small percent of whatever I recover for you. If I recover nothing, there will be no fee. So let us speak no more of money. Agreed?"

"Mrs. Wardell," Steve told them, "is in this all the way. She said for me to take all the time I want and to use a Half Diamond H horse till I get my roan back."

"My own money," Ron Garroway revealed, "is in a bank at Lamar, Colorado. Some day I hope to start a small stock ranch with it. Wasn't any use bringing it along when I came here just to give myself up."

"Speaking of ranches," Steve put in, "Lem Hopper took another prospective buyer out to the Wardell place yesterday."

"I don't like the idea," Christine worried, "of Ron going to Wickenburg. Not till his arm heals."

"No danger," Ron argued. "That fellow Rood doesn't know me. He won't have any idea what I'm after. I can find out what people think of him down there, get a slant on whether or not he's on the level. At least I can find out if Granby called on him during the last few days."

"Everybody," Christine complained, "has something to do except me! And it's all for my benefit."

"Your assignment," Gonzales said, "will be to watch Frank Maxwell."

The girl stared. "But why should I watch Mr. Maxwell?"

The lawyer turned to Ron. "You tell her, Ronaldo."

"At Simms' Camp," Ron reminded them, "Maxwell was robbed by a footpad. The thief cleaned out his wallet and threw it away along with a passbook on a St. Louis bank. The book showed a savings deposit of twenty-three thousand dollars made four days earlier. Maxwell lied about going to St. Louis, claimed he didn't go further east than Kansas City. Now it turns out that Isaac Pendleton lives in St. Louis."

"Perhaps a coincidence," Gonzales admitted. "But if it is not, then there is a connection between Maxwell and Pendleton. That, added to the fact that Maxwell is attorney for the Skyline mine, makes him well worth our attention."

An oddly embarrassed look appeared on Christine's face. "And only yesterday," she told them, "he asked me to go to the theater with him. To see *H. M. S. Pinafore*. And I turned him down."

"The next time he asks you for a date," Ricardo suggested, "please accept. We must learn all we can about Señor Maxwell. Also about Señores Pendleton, Granby, and Rood. Now I shall go out to buy tickets. For myself a round trip ticket to St. Louis by stage and train; and a round trip stagecoach ticket to Wickenburg for Ronaldo."

Early the next morning Steve saddled Shorty's sorrel at Shull's Livery stable. He tied a blanket roll back of the cantle and took the Granite Creek trail south out of

134

town. The crow-flight distance to Granby was only eighteen miles, but the twisting mountain route made the distance nearer twenty-five. After passing Bert Young's sawmill, he took the Walnut Grove trail through an upsloping forest of ponderosas. He'd never been to Granby, but he knew the smelter settlement was only about three miles up Milk Creek from Walnut Grove.

His saddle scabbard had a Winchester carbine and his gunbelt carried a Colt forty-five. There could be rough customers at a spot like Granby, gamblers and parasites preying on mine and smelter hands there. Nor could Steve forget that two of his personal enemies were loose in the woods somewhere: Ernie Jacks and Cass Pomeroy. Joe Walker had given him a warrant for each man, just in case. His temporary deputy ship was still in force.

By midmorning he had crossed a divide between the water-sheds of Granite Creek and the Hassayampa. From here the trail led downward. He passed two small mines, one active and one abandoned. At midday he struck upper Milk Creek and found only a thin flow of water there. Turning downcreek in a narrow canyon, he came suddenly out of the trees into the settlement of Granby.

It was strung out for half a mile between two high ridges. He knew that the one on the south divided it from Blind Indian Creek and that on its backbone was the fabulous producer called the Skyline mine. Had it originally been staked out nine years ago by Adam Mayberry?

A black smokestack marked the Granby smelter, and above it on the south Steve could see a steep trail leading down from shafts on the ridge and from tunnels on the slope. Ore-laden carts were coming down that slope to the smelter. A raucous grinding of machinery came from the smelter, and beyond it log and frame structures, some with sheet-iron roofs, lined either side of the gulch for half a mile.

Steve rode by the smelter and found three two-story buildings — a saloon, a store, and what passed for a hotel. A long, shabby building further on had a sign: *Amy Kelly: Board and Rooms.*

The hotel offered cots at fifty cents per night and a free corral back of it. Passing it up, he went on to a stable where hay was sold by the bale. He left the sorrel there and hurried to Amy Kelly's boarding house.

A dozen or more off-shift smelter hands were eating at a long table. Steve joined them and listened to their talk. It was disgruntled talk about an employer they called Old Squeeze-Penny. "We orter walk out on him," a man complained, "and try our luck over at Ed Peck's mine, I hear Ed's still payin' three-fifty."

Steve quickly became aware that they were talking about Chad Granby, who'd just reduced pay at the Skyline from $3.50 to $3.00 per day. Which offered Steve an atmosphere of discontent to work on. "Anybody seen a big blaze-face stallion up this way?" he asked them.

They hadn't. But it would do to explain why he was up here. He was obviously a ranch rider and might well be hunting for a valuable stray.

136

He picked two oldsters whose talk indicated that they'd been at the Skyline longer than the others and invited them to the saloon for beers. "This stray stallion's been gone a long time," he told them. "Might've been hit by lightnin'. Could be buzzard bait by now. Either of you fellas seen a horse skeleton out in the woods around here?"

Again they hadn't. Others joined them at the bar. By night Steve had asked more than thirty men if they'd seen the skeleton of a horse.

He slept on a cot at Amy Kelly's, and soon after sunup was riding toward the Skyline ridge. The winches of a dozen shafts were in sight there and well guarded to keep away outsiders. Ore carts were being loaded for haul down to the Milk Creek smelter. He easily found stone markers at the four corners of a claim — a rectangle fifteen hundred feet long by six hundred wide.

Had those four stone markers replaced wooden stakes, driven nine years ago by Adam Mayberry?

Had Mayberry been shot dead at about this spot, on a Sunday in 1873, and his body buried nearby? All through the fall of that year a sheriff had searched in vain for Mayberry. But the search had had no starting point. It had been haphazard and countrywide. Now Steve had an advantage not known to the 1873 sheriff. Whatever had happened had happened right about here. If Mayberry had been murdered by a claim jumper, his body would be buried not more than a mile from this spot.

After nine years of rains and snows there'd be little or no chance of finding it. That much Steve was willing to concede. But Mayberry had been mounted. His horse and saddle would be too bulky for burial by a murderer in a hurry to get far away from the scene of his crime.

What would I do myself? Steve reasoned. *I'd lead the saddled horse a couple of miles off into the hills, shoot it, and leave it in a thicket, maybe piling brush over it.*

All day he rode the area within a two-mile radius of the Skyline mine. He looked in every dense thicket and under every brushpile. He found the skeleton of a cow and the skull of an elk. But not the bones of a long-dead horse.

That night he again questioned disgruntled miners and smelter hands at Granby. For each of the next three days he rode the Skyline ridge, the wooded slopes on either side of it, and the gulches of Milk Creek and Blind Indian. Twice he found the skeleton of a burro. He found a dead mare, but there was too much flesh for the animal to have lain under the snows of nine winters. For three long days Steve rode the hills and brushy gulches, finding nothing which could have been the mount of Adam Mayberry.

The mount he did find was alive and hitched to the Granby store tie-rail at noon of the fourth day, when he rode back to Amy Kelly's for lunch. It was his own saddled roan — the animal on which Ernie Jacks had escaped at the Groom Creek cabin. Ernie's shotgun was tied to the saddle strings.

He went into the store and found Ernie at the counter buying a slab of bacon. The man was bone-thin and ragged from hiding out in the hills.

"You won't need it," Steve told him. "They'll feed you at the Prescott jail."

He drew his gun, exposed his badge, searched Ernie for a weapon. There was nothing but a knife. The half-starved little fugitive offered no resistance. He even managed a grin. "Jail grub won't be too bad," he admitted, "after livin' on rabbits for a week."

Steve took him to Amy Kelly's table for a quick meal. By one o'clock they were on their way to Prescott, Steve riding his own roan and Ernie on the sorrel.

They'd barely cleared the Granby settlement when Ernie, his hunger appeased now, offered a sly proposition. "What'll yuh take, Mulgrave, to turn me loose?"

"Nothing you could offer, Jacks."

"How do yuh know what I've got to offer, Mister Lawman? I hear talk at the store about what you been doin' the last few days. Folks say you're out lookin' for a horse that's been nine years dead."

"That's right. Don't tell me you know where I can find one."

"I sure do," Ernie claimed. "And I'll lead yuh right there if you'll turn me loose."

"No trade." Steve was certain that it was a subterfuge of some kind, anything that would make him ride in any other direction than toward the county jail.

"On my second night out from Groom Crik," Ernie insisted, "I hid in a chokecherry thicket. Brushiest

139

patch I could find anywhere. Reckon somebody else thought so too, when he shot a horse there long time ago."

"Found the skeleton of a horse, did you? What makes you think it was shot?"

"There was a hole through the skull, right between the eye sockets. I shook the skull and heard somethin' rattle. Shook it out and it was a rifle bullet. Just what you been lookin' for, mister."

Steve called an abrupt halt. There was a bare chance that Ernie was telling the truth. If so, the trade he offered was worth looking into. "Did you see an old saddle somewhere nearby?"

"Nope. Didn't see no saddle gear. Only a long-dead horse with a rifle slug in its skull."

The killer, Steve reasoned, after leading a saddled horse several miles from where he'd buried Mayberry, would shoot the horse in the densest thicket he could find, and then carry the saddle gear perhaps a hundred yards to another thicket so that if found it wouldn't necessarily be identified with the dead horse.

The main object was to build up Christine's case against the Granby-Pendleton-Rood combination. The case against Ernie was relatively unimportant. He was only wanted for assault and battery on Ron Garroway, and for an attempted extortion which hadn't succeeded.

"If you'll lead me to that thicket," Steve decided, "and if what you claim you saw is there, I'll turn you loose."

"With a bronc and saddle?" Ernie begged.

140

"No. On foot. A day's walk will take you to Gilette, and they need muckers there. Either that or come along to the county jail."

It was a hard bargain but Ernie took it. "Okay. It's about three mile from here, up Blind Indian."

An hour's ride took them over the Skyline ridge and down into Blind Indian gulch. There Ernie turned upstream. Steve followed, dubiously, and another half-hour took them beyond the orbit of his own search.

Wild chokecherry patches began appearing along the thin water run. Now, at the end of May, the trees were in full bloom.

At an especially dense thicket Ernie reined to a stop. "This is it. I holed up here like a coyote my second night outa Groom Crik."

Steve saw broken limbs where the fugitive had led his mount into the thicket. And in the very heart of the thicket lay the white bones of a horse. The ribs were still arched, but the skull had become detached. He looked closely at the skull. A hole between the eye sockets could have been made by a bullet. "You shook the bullet out, Jacks? What did you do with it?"

"Didn't touch it. Just left it lay where it fell."

With a closer look Steve saw the bullet. It lay right beside the skull. It might have been fired by an old rimfire 1866 Winchester forty-four rifle. The late centerfire forty-four-forties, he knew, hadn't been in use as early as 1873.

"A deal's a deal," Ernie reminded him. "You gotta leave me go now."

He'd given his word, so there was nothing he could do but keep it. He pointed southeast. "Bumblebee and Gilette are that way." He pointed west. "Walnut Grove is that way. Or you could head south toward Wickenburg. Take your choice."

Ernie lost no time and was soon out of sight. Nor was Steve sorry to be rid of him. Unmounted, the man would surely be picked up sooner or later. The thing now was to find the saddle gear which had been on this horse.

So far there was no proof that the animal had been Adam Mayberry's. Any horse bitten by a rattlesnake or breaking its leg in a badger hole would need to be shot.

This particular cherry patch covered perhaps an acre. Steve beat through it but could find no saddle gear. He saw sign that Ernie Jacks and his mount had bedded down here several nights ago. Then he looked upcreek a little way and saw a patch of wild plum which was also in bloom.

He led his two horses there and in less than fifteen minutes found the shabby, weathered remains of an old saddle. A bridle and moth-eaten saddle pad lay nearby. The leather parts had been gnawed by pack rats and the metal parts were coated with rust. Tied back of the saddle cantle was a black rubber raincoat in a tight roll. The saddle bags were empty. So, it seemed at first, were the pockets of the rubber coat.

Then Steve's fumbling fingers touched a pasteboard card in the depths of a coat pocket. When he took it out, it looked like an advertising card. On it was the picture of a steamship. This was about the last thing

Steve would have expected to find deep in the Arizona mountains.

Printing over the ship said:

The Colorado River Steam Navigation Company
San Francisco, California

Printing under the picture said

The Steamship NEWBERN, 943 tons; Captain Wm. McDonough
Plying between San Francisco and Port Isabel
First Class Fare, $75.00
Sailing time, 12 days   Next sailing, June 14, 1873

That was all. But it was enough.

For Port Isabel was at the top of the Gulf of California and at the mouth of the Colorado River. It was the route, and the very ship, and the exact sailing by which Adam Mayberry had arrived in Arizona.

CHAPTER
THIRTEEN

Ricardo Gonzales came out of the Planters' Hotel in St. Louis, where he'd just registered, and got into a two-horse hack waiting at the curb. "Where to?" the hackman asked.

Gonzales looked at a card on which he'd scribbled an address before leaving Prescott. It was a residence on King's Highway. He gave it to the hackman, and the cab was soon rolling that way. "It's a right good neighborhood," the hackman said. "You a stranger in St. Louee?"

The Arizona lawyer admitted that he was. This was the first time in his life that he'd ever been east of Santa Fe.

King's Highway proved to be a broad, maple-lined residential street paved with asphalt. The houses along it were more or less pretentious, some with balconies and well-kept lawns back of cast-iron fences. In general an upper-class neighborhood. Yet the house in front of which the cabman drew up was a cottage with only a picket fence. It was neat and freshly painted, but without the lilac and rose shrubbery conspicuous in adjacent yards.

Gonzales paid and dismissed the driver. A mailbox at the cottage gate had the name Jerome Lambert over it. This was to be expected. For six years the treasurer of the Skyline mining company had been mailing monthly checks to Isaac Pendleton at this address. Upon selling out and retiring in 1876, Pendleton had notified the mine officials that he'd thereafter be living with a St. Louis nephew named Jerome Lambert.

Gonzales went up a brick walk to a porch and knocked at the cottage door. He had to knock twice before it was opened. A sleepy-eyed man in a dressing gown stood there. He was middle-aged and overweight, with a flabby face and pale, moist eyes. The untidiness of a hallway back of him gave Gonzales the idea that the place had no female housekeeper.

"Are you Mr. Jerome Lambert?"

The man nodded. "What do you want?"

"A word with your uncle, Mr. Pendleton."

Right away there was a change. Sleepy indolence on the man's face was replaced by a taut caution. "Uncle Ike's gone fishing," he said.

"May I ask where? I've come a long way to see him."

"Yeh? How long a way?"

"From Prescott, Arizona."

Now there was something more than caution in the man's moist blue eyes. His answer came in a crack which might be nervousness or even fright. "Too bad you missed Uncle Ike. He's down in the Ozarks fishing somewhere."

"When will he be back?"

"No telling. Sometimes he stays out all summer. Used to be a prospector, and he likes to rough it."

"Where do you forward his mail?"

"I don't. I hold it till he comes back. Wouldn't know where to send it. Sometimes he's down on the Gasconnade, sometimes on White River. Last summer he went clear to Arkansas."

"So there's no way I can find him?" Gonzales prodded.

"Not till he gets back. Hard to find Uncle Ike after the bass start biting."

"He's here all winter, though?"

"Most of the time. Last winter he went to New Orleans for a couple of weeks; winter before last he warmed himself up at Palm Beach for a while."

"And you never know where to forward his mail?"

"Nope. I just hold it till he gets back."

"Thanks. Sorry I bothered you." With a disarming smile Gonzales turned and went back to the street. He moved along the walk until he was beyond sight of the cottage.

Then he stood for a while under a maple tree in shrewd thought. It didn't seem logical that a man who was receiving a check for a thousand dollars a month would go away on long trips without leaving a forwarding address. Or that his nephew would be completely out of touch with him for long periods of time.

There was a simple answer, improbable but quite possible. After milling it over, he went back to a house next door to the Jerome Lambert cottage. His knock brought an elderly housekeeper to the door.

"Excuse me. I'm looking for Mr. Isaac Pendleton. I'm told he lives in this block but I've lost the exact address."

"You mean old Ike Pendleton?" the woman exclaimed. "Only Ike Pendleton I ever knew lived next door." She nodded toward the Lambert cottage. "But he's been dead four years. Died of a heart stroke back in seventy-eight."

"Are you sure?"

"Of course I'm sure. Stood right here in this doorway and saw the hearse haul him away. Why don't you go next door and ask his nephew Jerry Lambert?"

"Thank you. I will."

But first the lawyer from Arizona checked with a neighbor on the other side of the cottage. This time the man of the house himself confirmed it. "Went to the funeral myself," the man remembered. "Knew Ike well. He and I used to play checkers. What made you think he's still living?"

Ricardo shrugged, not bothering to explain. He knew now that for the last forty-eight months endorsements had been forged on as many thousand-dollar checks. By the nephew, of course. The Skyline treasurer had the cancelled checks on file. By the terms under which Isaac Pendleton had sold out to Granby, the annuity would continue only through the seller's lifetime. Therefore the nephew had by now defrauded the Skyline company out of forty-eight thousand dollars.

Again he knocked at the Lambert cottage. Again a short delay before Jerome Lambert opened the door. He was still in dressing gown and slippers, and the look of nervous fright was still on his face.

"I've just found out," Ricardo said, "that your uncle died four years ago."

The man wilted into abject hopelessness. His shoulders sagged, and he didn't even offer a denial. "I always knew someone would find out someday."

"May I come in?"

Lambert stood aside and let the lawyer in. There was a seldom-used parlor off the hall, and Gonzales sat on a sofa there. Jerome Lambert slumped into a chair and stared dully into space.

"What made you do it?" Gonzales prompted.

"I only meant to do it once," the man said wretchedly. "Just one month, I mean. When I got back from the funeral there was a check from Arizona in the mailbox. I couldn't bear to send it back."

"So you practiced your uncle's signature and cashed it."

The man gave a glum nod. "Then I meant to notify Mr. Granby that my uncle was dead so he wouldn't need to keep up the annuity. I kept putting it off. Next month another check came. I endorsed and cashed it. After that it was too late to stop."

"Did your uncle ever mention the name Adam Mayberry to you? Or an assayer named Harley Rood?"

"No. He never mentioned anyone except Mr. Granby. Said Granby had grubstaked him fifty-fifty and they wound up half-and-half owners of a silver mine."

148

To Gonzales Lambert's responses seemed forthright and convincing. The truth was out now and the man knew it; he'd given up all attempt at deception.

"A few weeks ago the mine's attorney, Frank Maxwell, came to St. Louis. Did he call on you?"

To this question Lambert made no response at all. In his mood of complete despondency he may not even have heard it. Gonzales had his own definite idea about it. The $23,000 Maxwell had deposited in a St. Louis bank was approximately half the total sum illegally collected by Lambert.

"You've cashed forty-eight annuity checks since your uncle's death."

"About that many. It's been four years. You'll report me to the police?"

"I'll have to," Gonzales said. "It's grand larceny, and I'll be an accessory after the fact if I fail to report it. And since the crime was committed in St. Louis, I'll have to report it here."

Jerome Lambert buried his fleshy face in his arms. A moan of despair escaped him. "I don't want to go to prison."

"None of us do, Mr. Lambert." Gonzales left him and went out to the street. He walked briskly till he came to a streetcar corner. A cable car came along and he rode it downtown, where he was directed to police headquarters.

"I've just stumbled on a forty-eight-thousand-dollar larceny," he reported to a police captain. He gave details of Lambert's guilt.

"If you need me I'll be at the Planters' Hotel."

A long stagecoach ride from Prescott to Canyon Diablo followed by more than a thousand miles on trains had tired Ricardo Gonzales so that when he got to his hotel room he was soon soundly asleep. He slept the rest of the day and night. He was at breakfast the next morning when he saw a front page headline.

SUICIDE ON KING'S HIGHWAY
SELF-HANGED FELON CHEATS PRISON

When police arrived to arrest Jerome Lambert for stealing forty-eight thousand dollars, they found him hanging from a rafter in his backyard barn. He had stood on a barrel to noose his neck, then kicked the barrel out from under him. The felony had just been exposed an hour earlier by an Arizona attorney, Ricardo Gonzales. Lambert choosing death rather than prison, left no note . . .

Gonzales laid the paper aside with a sigh. It was now too late to question the man further about the origin of an 1873 silver strike. Or about Frank Maxwell's recent trip to St. Louis. There was nothing he could do except book passage back to Arizona.

CHAPTER
FOURTEEN

Chad Granby, his wide, beardless face bloated with fury, looked at the sheaf of forty-eight cancelled checks which Joshua Finch had just handed him. Then he slammed them on his desk beside a pair of inquiring telegrams from the St. Louis police. He was a man with an undersized body and an oversized head, white-haired and white-eyebrowed. All his life he'd run roughshod over others, but now his usual cold calm had deserted him. The pitch of his anger had pumped blood to his cheeks, streaking them with purple veins.

In the office with him were Finch, his auditor, and his bodyguard, Alf Sligo.

"We can't prosecute Pendleton's nephew," Granby fumed, "because he's dead. But what about Frank Maxwell?"

"I've talked with people who came in on the stage with Maxwell," Finch reported. "They say that at Simms' Camp he was robbed by a footpad who threw away what he couldn't use. One item was a savings account passbook on a St. Louis bank showing a twenty-three-thousand-dollar deposit made four days earlier. Maxwell had made a business trip to Kansas City, denying that he'd gone any farther east."

151

"So it's open and shut," Granby glowered. "You agree?"

The auditor didn't. "No sir, because we can't really prove anything. Personally I've no doubt as to what happened. As our attorney, Maxwell became suspicious that Pendleton was no longer living. So he made a side trip from Kansas City to St. Louis, checking at Pendleton's address. No doubt the nephew told him that Uncle Ike had gone fishing or hunting somewhere. But like Gonzales did later, Maxwell inquired of neighbors and learned the truth."

"But instead of reporting to the police," Granby concluded bitterly, "as Gonzales did, Maxwell held him up for half the loot! Twenty-four thousand dollars. Pocketed a thousand and hid the rest in a St. Louis savings account." The owner of the Skyline mine whipped around to Sligo. "Send word to Maxwell," he demanded, "that I want to see him right away."

Maxwell's office was only a block away, on the east side of the plaza. In ten minutes the lawyer, meticulously groomed as usual, was ushered into Granby's presence. Tall, muscular, with just enough wine red in his cheeks to make him look distinguished, he came in with an air of being cocksure of himself. Not until he saw that the auditor, Finch, and the gunslung Sligo were also in the office did he lose a little of his aplomb.

"What's up, chief?"

"Twenty-four thousand dollars!" Granby bellowed. "The bribe Lambert slipped you for not giving him away. What did you do with it?"

The lawyer's attempt at a confused stare wasn't quite successful. "A bribe? Lambert? Who's Lambert? Never heard of him."

"Don't try to play innocent, Maxwell. Where did you get the twenty-three thousand you put in a St. Louis savings account?"

"That? It was a long overdue fee I collected from a client."

"The name of the client?"

"He prefers not to be mentioned. And I shall respect the confidential lawyer-client relationship."

The brazenness of it made Granby boil over. "I'll sue you for it," he stormed.

"That," Maxwell admitted with a shrug, "is your privilege."

"As for right now," Granby roared, "you're fired. You're no longer attorney for the Skyline. And I'll see to it you never get another case in Yavapai County."

"If you defame me without proof," Maxwell countered, "I in turn will sue you. And get a judgment. Is that all, Mr. Granby?"

"Not quite. I'm giving you twenty-four hours to hand me back half the money Ike Pendleton's nephew swindled me out of. If you don't come clean, I'll have Sligo take it out of your crooked, thieving hide. Now get out."

When the stagecoach from End-of-Track arrived at three that afternoon, a weary Ricardo Gonzales alighted from it. Steve Mulgrave, half expecting him, was waiting in front of the Williams House.

153

"You heard about what happened in St. Louis, Estevan?"

Steve nodded. "The St. Louis police sent a flock of telegrams to Chad Granby, checking up. He's chewing nails, Granby is, and they say he's fired Frank Maxwell."

"What about young Garroway? Is he back from Wickenburg?"

"Not yet. I look for him on this evening's stage from the south. The big news is that I found the skeleton of Adam Mayberry's horse in a thicket up Blind Indian gulch. And Mayberry's saddle not too far away." Steve showed the lawyer a rifle bullet taken from a horse's skull and a card advertising an 1873 voyage made by the steamship *Newbern*.

Gonzales looked at the exhibits and asked for details. When he had them, he gave a shrewd nod. "More and more it looks like a Granby-Pendleton-Rood conspiracy, Estevan. Has anything else happened since I left here?"

"Nothing except that Mrs. Wardell has finally found a buyer for her ranch."

"Yes? Who?" All the while Steve and Gonzales were walking toward the bank building. They went up narrow stairs and into the lawyer's office.

"The sale is being made," Steve said, "through a real estate agency representing the buyer. Makes no difference because it's a cash deal. The deed's being made out to the Skull Valley Livestock Company, Incorporated. Never heard of that outfit. Chances are the main stockholder is some easterner who wants to try his hand raisin' cattle. He's buying it at a fair price,

154

so he won't lose any money. Cow business is just getting started in this county. He can probably sell out in a year and make a profit."

"Which leaves you and Shorty and Lem without jobs," Ricardo suggested.

"Except Mrs. Wardell wants Shorty and me to keep baching in the backyard cabin long as we're workin' on the Mayberry case. I'll draw pay as a county deputy, and Lem can go to work for a Lonesome Valley outfit anytime he wants to. Meantime Lem's holding down the Half Diamond H till the new buyer moves in."

"And how is my pretty little client, Christine?"

"She's brimful of excitement ever since I told her about what I found in Blind Indian gulch. And she's meeting every stage from Wickenburg, hoping Ron Garroway'll be on it." Steve looked at his watch. "I'll be with her when she meets the next one, in just three hours."

"Garroway will go to the Williams House?"

"Nope. Mrs. Wardell invited him to bunk with Shorty and me in the backyard cabin. She's as excited as Christine about the Mayberry case. Wants you to show up for supper tonight and talk it over. And Ron too, if he gets in from Wickenburg. Wants you and Ron to bring us up to date on everything."

At six o'clock Ricardo Gonzales presented himself at Emily Wardell's town house, and by half past six had given her a full account of his St. Louis adventure. Emily in turn told the lawyer about the latest Prescott sensation — Chad Granby's discharging Frank Maxwell as counsel for the Skyline company. "He's

155

sure Maxwell got half of the money, but most people think he'll never be able to prove it."

Gonzales shrugged. "If our thought about a conspiracy is correct, it's a case of one thief stealing from another. Estevan tells me you have a buyer for your ranch."

"Yes. A cash sale to a corporation."

"And you had already sold the chattel?"

"The livestock and the ranching tools, yes. But the house furnishings go with the ranch. Except of course a few personal things, like books and family photographs. These I'd already brought to town with me. Isn't that a hack stopping in front?"

It was, and out of it came Christine, Steve, and Ron Garroway. Ron, who'd been a full week in Wickenburg, still had his left arm in a sling. Steve carried his bag for him as the three came into the house. Christine and Steve had met Ron at the stage depot and brought him directly here.

"And what," Gonzales asked after greetings, "did you find at Wickenburg?"

"Not as much," Ron confessed, "as you did at St. Louis."

"You saw Harley Rood?"

"Yes, but could get nothing out of him. He won't admit that Granby called on him a few days before I got there."

"We may be sure he did," Gonzales insisted. "He would go secretly to Rood's house by night. Perhaps just to warn him that Adam Mayberry's daughter had arrived after nine years with knowledge that her father staked a claim on a certain ridge."

"I put up at the Arizona Hotel," Ron told them. "It's the only hotel there. The registry book shows the names of Chadwick Granby and Alf Sligo a few days before I got there. They only stopped one night and then drove back to Prescott. No way to prove they ever saw Rood."

Christine's face showed disappointment. Gonzales gave a shrug and a sigh. "So it was a waste of time, sending you down there."

"Maybe not," Ron corrected. "I asked the editor of the Wickenburg weekly *Times* to let me see his old files. He told me to help myself. In a nine-year-old issue, dated September, eighteen seventy-three, I found a mention of Harley Rood and copied it down. Listen." He brought out a notebook and read from it:

"We are glad to welcome Mr. Harley Rood of Prescott, who during the past week has moved his assaying office to Wickenburg. Mr. Rood personally drove his equipment down here in an open wagon, making the eighty-four miles in three days. The first night out he stopped at Henry Wardell's ranch near Skull Valley, and the second night he stopped at the McCloud place on Date Creek . . ."

"Wait a minute!" An odd expression was dawning on Emily Wardell's face as she interrupted. "I vaguely remember now. People were always stopping overnight with us in those days. Skull Valley's twenty-six miles from Prescott on the Wickenburg road — just about as

157

far as a loaded wagon can get in one day. Hundreds of people must have stopped with us. Henry would never turn anyone down. Generally we just let them camp by the creek. But if they weren't equipped to camp, sometimes we gave them supper, bed, and breakfast at the house."

"You let Harley Rood stay at the house that time?" This sharply from Gonzales.

"We probably did. It's hard to be sure after nine years. But he was a prominent Prescott citizen, and my husband knew him, of course. If he was by himself, we almost surely let him sleep in the ranch house guest room."

"According to the newspaper," Ron said, "he made the drive to Wickenburg alone. Listen to the rest of it." He continued reading:

". . . Mr. Rood arrived with a bullet hole through his hat and four more bullet holes in the frame of his wagon. Someone emptied a rifle at him from ambush as he reached the head of Skull Valley Creek. A lurking Apache, no doubt. But Mr. Rood whipped his team to a run and made it safely to the Wardell ranch."

"Did he tell you," Steve asked his employer, "about being shot at?"

"Perhaps he told my husband. If he did Henry would conclude it was a shot by some renegade Apache. It happened often in those days."

Gonzales was less sure of it. "Let us think about that," he suggested. "If Isaac Pendleton jumped Adam Mayberry's claim and murdered him for the benefit of himself and Granby, the assayer Rood would know enough about it to make him a dangerous witness. They would have reason to silence him. Perhaps being fearful of them is why Rood moved to Wickenburg. It could be Pendleton who sniped at him on the way. Perhaps Granby and Pendleton could trust each other, but not Harley Rood."

Christine asked, "Is that all the paper said about Mr. Rood?"

"It's all the eighteen seventy-three paper said about him," Ron told her. "But nine years later, only a week ago, Harley Rood's name crops up again. Listen." He turned a page of his notebook to read another item. "This, mind you, happened on the night that Chad Granby and Alf Sligo were registered at the Wickenburg Hotel.

A mysterious holdup took place last night in the office of David Smedley, prominent Wickenburg attorney. He was working late when a masked man slipped in and held him up with a gun. The gunman told him to open the office safe. Since the safe contained no money, or anything at all of value to an outsider, Smedley opened it. The masked man then rapped him with the gun and knocked him unconscious. When the attorney came to, he looked to see what the robber had taken. To his surprise only one item was missing. It was a sealed envelope dated September, 1873, and labeled: 'This envelope contains the holograph will of Harley Rood, to be opened only in the event of his death.'"

CHAPTER
FIFTEEN

The name Harley Rood left them all gaping. It was a minute before the nimble brain of Ricardo Gonzales grasped the significance of two dates.

On his first day at Wickenburg, nine years ago, Rood had left a sealed envelope in a lawyer's safe. On Chad Granby's one night in Wickenburg, only a week ago, a masked man had recovered that envelope at the point of a gun.

"We must conclude," Ricardo reasoned, "that the gunman was Sligo."

"But why?" Steve puzzled. "Say the sealed envelope told tales on Granby. But Rood can now seal the same secret in another envelope and put it back in the same safe. So what does Granby gain by stealing it?"

For that Gonzales had no answer. "My only thought," he said, "is this: Rood was sure in his own mind nine years ago that Granby and Pendleton had tried to kill him. To stop them from trying again, he wrote down what happened to Adam Mayberry, sealed it in an envelope, and left it in a lawyer's safe immediately upon arriving in Wickenburg. The lawyer did not know, and still does not know, what was in the envelope. But by letter Rood could tell Granby what was in the envelope and that it would be opened after his death. That could make Granby and Pendleton decide to let Rood live in peace. Only after Christine arrives with proof that her father found and staked a claim where the Skyline mine is now, does Granby decide to seize the envelope by force."

They went in to a supper of chicken and dumplings. All during it, and later in the parlor, the three men and two women weighed the possibilities. Everything clicked except one unanswered question: What could Granby gain by stealing a sealed envelope which would immediately be replaced by another containing the same information?

It was after eleven when Gonzales left them and Steve and Ron went to their bunks in the backyard cabin.

Before they could drop off to sleep, Shorty Brill came in. He'd spent the evening at the Palace saloon on the plaza. "Didja hear the latest?" he asked them. "Happened right after dark and it's all over town by now."

"What?" Both Steve and Ron sat up curiously.

"Frank Maxwell got the livin' hell beat out of him. He was in his law office when some guy walked in and batted him over the head. When Maxie came to he was black and blue with a front tooth knocked out."

"Sligo?" The name came in one voice from Steve and Ron.

"Maybe," Shorty said. "All Maxwell says is that somebody came in and beat him up. He's in the hospital now and he's not accusin' anybody. Chances are he's got a pretty good idea who did it."

"So have I," Steve added confidently. "In this town you don't cheat Chad Granby out of twenty-four thousand dollars and get away with it. It's a cinch bet that Chad sent Sligo over there to bang down on him. Maxwell's lucky to be alive."

When Steve reported to the sheriff's office in the morning, Walker and two of his deputies were talking about Maxwell. "Must've been Sligo," Roy St. John agreed. "But we can't lay a finger on him so long as Maxwell doesn't make a complaint."

Sheriff Joe Walker got grimly to his feet. "One thing I can do. I can cancel that special deputyship Chad Granby wrangled for Sligo. I don't give a hang how much political pressure Chad brings on it; I'm not gonna carry any beat-'em-up thugs on my staff."

He was especially determined to do so when Steve told him about the masked man at Wickenburg who'd clubbed a lawyer there to steal a paper from a safe. No proof that it was Sligo, but Walker could hardly doubt it.

He left the courthouse and crossed Goodwin Street to the Skyline offices for a showdown with Sligo. When he came back, he had Sligo's special deputy badge in his hand. "Chad didn't raise any rumpus about it, either. All he did was alibi Sligo for the beat-up job on Maxwell. Said Sligo was in the office with him when it happened."

"Saw Chad in the bank yesterday," Deputy Herbert put in, "and he was hopping mad. You can't blame him much, after finding out he's been mailing a thousand dollars a month to a dead man the last four years. And his own lawyer grabbin' off half the take!"

"Which we can guess at but can't prove," Walker growled. "Anyway, whatever crooked stuff happened was in St. Louis, clear out of our jurisdiction."

District Attorney Ferd Oliver came into the office with certain opinions of his own.

"About this Mayberry case, Sheriff. I've gone over everything we've got so far, and this is what it adds up to: one, a long-lost letter from Mayberry to his wife reveals that he staked out a silver claim on a ridge where the Skyline is now; two, he left a rich sample from it with a Prescott assayer after dark on a Saturday night; three, at that time Chad Granby held an overdue mortgage on the property of an assayer named Harley Rood; four, early Sunday morning Mayberry rode back to his claim, whether by himself or accompanied by Pendleton and Granby we don't know; five, Mayberry was never seen again; six, soon after that Isaac Pendleton filed the Skyline claim as a fifty-fifty partnership with his grubstaker, Chad Granby; seven, Harley Rood never mentioned the ore sample left with him by Mayberry; eight, Granby never foreclosed the overdue mortgage on Rood's property; nine, a month later Rood moved to Wickenburg; ten, nine years later Mayberry's saddle is found not far from the Skyline mine, and close by the skeleton of a rifle-shot horse.

"All of which," Oliver summed up, "suggests but does not prove conspiracy to murder Mayberry and take over his claim. What I mean is, it's too loose a case for me to take any action on."

When Steve told about the seizure of a sealed envelope at Wickenburg, Oliver was impressed but still unconvinced. "It's still too loose. If you come up with anything else, Joe, let me know."

After Oliver left them, Joe Walker looked glumly at an array of reports on his desk. "We can't spend all our time on this Mayberry case, boys. There was a knifing last night at the Hassayampa Hangout. That joint gets meaner every day. Whenever the pickings begin to get poor at one of the construction camps along the railroad grade, some more bully boys drift down here to Prescott. The Hassayampa dive's crawlin' with 'em. I've spotted men in there who've served time for robbing coaches and trains. One of 'em's a guy named Lou Thatcher who was run out of Albuquerque after being tried twice for murder. Got off both times with rigged alibis. Mel Leonard thinks he's organizing a gang at the Hassayampa dump and we'd better keep an eye on him."

"Want us to go pick him up?" St. John offered.

Walker shook his head. "Not till we get the goods on him. You and Herbert make it a point to patrol the Hangout twice a day and once at night; if you get any proof of an organized gang we'll run a few of them in. I've got to send Kim Long to the grading camps. He can patrol back and forth between Flagstaff and Simms' Camp. Millard's already left for Gilette. Dead man found back of a saloon there — a dark-of-the-night gun job."

"What about me?" Steve asked.

"You," Walker decided, "had better stick with the Mayberry case. And keep an eye on Frank Maxwell. He's still got that twenty-three thousand dollars, and Granby's not likely to forget it."

"You think Sligo'll work him over again some night?"

"I'd bet on it. And next time it could be with a gun."

When Steve went to the Wardell house at noon, Emily Wardell met him with news. "The ranch sale was closed this morning, Steve. I've just banked the check."

"Who signed it?"

"The Skull Valley Livestock Company, Incorporated, which is the name on the deed. They can take possession any time they want."

In the afternoon Steve called at the hospital and found that Maxwell had been discharged and sent home. On his way back to the plaza he looked in at the Hassayampa Hangout. The bar was lined with rowdies, and it didn't take him long to pick out Lou Thatcher. A bulky man with thin hair and a scar on his swarthy left cheek. His gunbelt was full of brass cartridges, but the holster was empty. Steve couldn't doubt that the gun wasn't far away, probably where the bartender could toss it to its owner at any minute. Thatcher was bragging about something he'd once done at Trinidad, Colorado, but stopped abruptly when Steve came in. Steve drank a short beer and left. The instant he was

166

outside a chorus of laughs came from the bar. A voice said, "And you kin count me in on it, Thatch."

Steve patrolled Whiskey Row and found it relatively quiet. At the Nifty he bought Jimmie-Behind-the-Stove a drink. At four o'clock he called at Chad Granby's upstairs office and found the mine owner at his desk, with Sligo lounging in a corner of the room. Sligo had been gunless and badgeless since early morning, and it showed in his temper. "Who invited *you* in here?" he snarled as Steve appeared in the doorway.

"Invited myself in," Steve said cheerily.

"And what," Chad Granby demanded, "did you expect to find?"

"Not a horse skull with a rifle bullet in it. I already found that — and pretty close to the Skyline mine. Nor a saddle once ridden up there by a man who came here on the *Newbern*. I already found that too — and not far from the Skyline. So I keep looking for something else; maybe a sealed envelope with murder proof in it." Needling Granby, Steve was hoping, might jar him into a false move.

"Get out of here!" Chad Granby bellowed it with his face flaming.

Steve went back to Joe Walker's courthouse office and found it empty. But a telegram from Tucson was there, just delivered from the Fort Whipple military telegraph office. It was from the sheriff of Pima County announcing that Cass Pomeroy had been picked up there with about fifteen thousand in currency on him.

Which meant that either Walker himself or one of his deputies must go on a long stage ride to Maricopa, and thence on a Southern Pacific train to Tucson, to take charge of the prisoner and bring him back to Prescott. Would he be hanged, Steve wondered, like Crocker and Stallings?

At sundown he went to John Shull's livery stable with a reminder. "Don't forget, John, if Chad Granby and his man Sligo leave town, you're to let me know right away. Chad still keeps his buckboard here, doesn't he."

"That's right, Steve. Uses it for a trip to the Skyline every once in a while. I'll tip you if he leaves town with it."

The tip came sooner than expected. Steve had been asleep less than half an hour that night when a messenger tapped on the door of Emily Wardell's backyard cabin. Ron and Steve were there, but Shorty Brill was down on the plaza somewhere.

The message was from Shull. Steve lighted an oil lamp to read it. "Granby and Sligo just pulled out of here, dressed for a long night ride."

"Heading for the Skyline mine, do you suppose?" Ron wondered.

"Maybe," Steve said. "Or maybe for Wickenburg to deal with Rood. The best bet is he went to the mine. He keeps a private cabin at Granby. Goes there coupla times a month to see his mine and smelter foremen. But I never knew him to make the drive at night. It's a rough mountain trail — not the kind you'd want to drive at night."

"I'm betting on Wickenburg," Ron argued. "Maybe one of us had better tag along after him."

"I'll leave it up to Joe Walker," Steve decided. He dressed, walked the few blocks to the sheriff's house, and told him about Granby.

"Trailin' him by night's no good," Walker concluded. "Maybe he went to Granby, maybe to Wickenburg — or maybe to the A & P railhead to catch a train for St. Louis. Might want to file a suit in St. Louis to get back money from the estate of Ike Pendleton's nephew. Might even have gone to Camp Verde or Gilette or Bumblebee to collect a debt. People all over the county owe money to Chad Granby."

So Steve went back to bed. In the morning he inquired at the Skyline offices, but no one there would admit knowing where Granby and his bodyguard had gone.

The answer came late in the afternoon when Lem Hopper came into town after a twenty-six-mile ride from the Half Diamond H. "The new buyer showed up," he reported to Steve and Emily Wardell. "Showed me his title deed and moved in. Told me to get the hell out of there. He fetched along a buckboard load of groceries like he aimed to stay quite a spell."

"Who?" Steve and Emily asked in a breath.

"He had papers to show he's president of the Skull Valley Livestock Company — and a gunslung bodyguard. Owns half the county, I've heard. Man by the name of Chad Granby."

CHAPTER
SIXTEEN

Again there was a strategy meeting held in Emily Wardell's parlor. Present were Steve, Ron, Christine, and Ricardo Gonzales — with Emily serving coffee and cookies. It was at nightfall of the day Lem Hopper had turned the Half Diamond H over to its new owner.

"But he's a millionaire mine operator," Emily exclaimed, "a money lender and . . . well, just about everything except a cattle rancher. Why would he want my Skull Valley ranch?"

Gonzales had already asked himself that question and had come up with an answer. "Because," he concluded, "it was there that Harley Rood spent a night in your guest room nine years ago.

"I don't get it," Ron said. Others in the room were equally confused. "He need take no money loss," Gonzales went on, "in buying the ranch. He knows the value of Yavapai County ranch land, and so it won't be a losing speculation. When it has served his purpose, he can sell it for as much as he paid for it."

"And what," Christine asked, "*is* his purpose?"

"To live there long enough," the attorney answered confidently, "to find a message Harley Rood planted that night."

"But the message," Ron objected, "was planted in a sealed envelope at Wickenburg."

"Not necessarily," Gonzales argued. "Put yourself in the place of Harley Rood as he drove his wagon out of Prescott nine years ago. Near the end of the first day you get to the head of Skull Valley Creek on your way to Wickenburg. A rifleman snipes at you from a gulch — five shots, one through your hat and four thumping into the frame of your wagon. Maybe you see the sniper; anyway you're sure he's Ike Pendleton, killer of Adam Mayberry, sent by Chad Granby to waylay you because of what you know. You whip to a gallop, arriving safely at the Wardell ranch where they let you stay all night."

That much was easy to understand. "I dimly remember," Emily said, "that we were eating supper when he arrived."

"Did he look scared," Steve asked, "like he'd just been shot at?"

"After nine years I can't say, Steve. He may have confided in my husband. Henry knew him well and probably went down to the barn to help him unhitch. He would then take the guest to the guest room. If Henry tabbed it as shots from a spiteful Apache on the loose, he wouldn't want to alarm me with it. I was probably in the kitchen serving when Harley Rood sat down to eat."

"The certain thing is," Gonzales reasoned, "that Rood was alone all night in a guest room. He'd expected the sniper to try again; so he might never reach Wickenburg alive. What could he do about it?

171

Rood couldn't call in the law because he was guilty himself — although to what degree we don't know. But he could write and plant a statement which when found would convict both Pendleton and Granby. I believe he did. He wrote it during those nine hours he spent in your ranch house guest room, Mrs. Wardell. Before driving on toward Wickenburg in the morning he secreted it in a place where it would later be found. Maybe in that guest room, maybe elsewhere in the house, maybe in the barn or an outbuilding while he was hitching up the next morning. My belief is that it is still there."

"The guest room," Emily said, "has an iron bed with hollow bedposts. You mean some place like a bedpost?"

"That is one of a hundred possibilities," Ricardo agreed. "Now let us go on with Harley Rood as he proceeds toward Wickenburg. He arrives at the end of the third day and by then realizes that the planted message may never be found."

The lawyer waited till Christine had refilled his coffee cup, then continued. "He doesn't want it found in his lifetime. But if he is murdered by Pendleton or some other agent of Granby, he wants it found immediately."

"So he rewrites the message," Christine suggested, "and puts it in a sealed envelope."

"That was my first thought," Ricardo admitted. "That he labeled the envelope as enclosing a will, although actually it contained only a statement of Adam Mayberry's murder and the jumping of a claim. Now I do not think so. More likely the sealed envelope at Wickenburg contained only a key to a hiding place. A statement something like this: 'In the event of my death by violence, look for a full explanation at the Henry Wardell ranch near Skull Valley.' Perhaps no more than just that. But after planting the sealed envelope in a lawyer's safe, which we know was the first thing Rood did after arriving at Wickenburg, he wrote to Granby warning him that assassination would immediately be followed by exposure."

"It'd make Granby lay off of him," Steve agreed.

"Yes — for the next nine years till Christine arrived with a long-lost letter. A letter which reveals that her father staked a claim at or near Granby's silver bonanza on the Milk Creek ridge. It builds a fire under Granby, so he drives to Wickenburg to see Rood. After nine years Rood is a little less frightened than he was in eighteen seventy-three. He again warns Granby that his assassination will be followed by exposure; a lawyer will open his safe to look at a dead man's will — finding instead the key to murder guilt, both his own and Mayberry's."

"So Granby," Steve added, "has Sligo steal the sealed envelope. After reading what was in it, Granby came back to Prescott and bought the ranch."

"It gives him possession," Ricardo explained, "while he searches for a message there. He'll need plenty of time. It won't be easily or quickly found, else one of your own household, Mrs. Wardell, would have stumbled on it long ago."

"He knew the ranch was for sale at a fair price," Emily said, "so someone was sure to buy it sooner or later. Any new owner moving in might find the message; a risk Granby didn't want to take."

"We now know," Gonzales resumed, "why Granby insisted that chattel be included with the land. House furniture, bar equipment, hay machinery — everything except livestock, which had already been sold. We can be sure he's sifting through those things right now. Another point is cleared up too. We wondered why Granby would bother to steal a sealed envelope which could immediately be replaced by another containing the same information. Now it is different. The danger to Granby isn't in the sealed envelope. The envelope isn't a hazard so long as Harley Rood lives; he's still under fifty and will probably outlive Chad Granby. The real danger to Granby is at the Wardell ranch; so he neutralizes it by taking legal possession."

"And there's nothing we can do about it?" Ron wondered.

"Not a thing, Ronaldo. It is his property, and he can tear it apart stone by stone and board by board if he wants to. If in a few weeks he puts the ranch back on the market, we will know he has found what he is looking for and has destroyed it."

"He has many other important affairs," Emily reminded them. "A rich silver mine, a smelter, a loan business here in town . . . so he can't stay out at the ranch all the time."

"That is true," Gonzales agreed. "He will perhaps come in once a week to sign papers and make decisions; then he will go back to Skull Valley and resume search for what Rood planted there. Always with his bodyguard close by. Does anyone else have a thought on this?"

No one did, and the meeting broke up.

Early in the morning Steve saw Sheriff Joe Walker board a southbound coach. "As I go through Wickenburg, Steve, I'll drop in on Harley Rood. We can't lay a hand on him yet. But if I shoot him a few fast questions he might give something away."

"What kind of questions, Sheriff?"

"Like does he know why Chad Granby bought the Wardell ranch and moved out there. Maybe it'll faze him and maybe it won't. I'll only have thirty minutes at Wickenburg."

The stagecoach would then go on south another hundred miles beyond Wickenburg to a connection with the Southern Pacific railroad, whose transcontinental track had just been completed. A train would take Walker east to Tucson, from where he'd return with the prisoner Cass Pomeroy.

The coach pulled out and Steve walked back to the courthouse basement office, where he found Roy St. John. "Anything new come in, Roy?"

"A quiet night on Whiskey Row, Mel Leonard tells me. Another rumpus at the Hassayampa Hangout, but we don't know who started it. Another big bullion shipment went through yesterday from the Skyline smelter. Kim Long's still patrollin' the grading camps and Millard hasn't got back from Gilette."

"As I crossed the plaza," Steve said, "I ran into Frank Maxwell. Looked kinda down in the mouth."

"And no wonder!" St. John said. "They say he's losin' his clients, one by one. Chad Granby fired him and everybody knows why. So the three biggest stores in town have quit him. Head's, Goldwater's, and Bashford's. For years he's done most of their law work. But after hearing how he gypped Granby, they gave him the sack."

During that day and the next still other clients deserted Maxwell. Mines and merchants he'd served professionally lost no time in severing connections with a lawyer who, according to what seemed more than guesswork, had cheated the Skyline company out of $24,000.

Steve heard talk about it along Whiskey Row. "Nobody'll ever trust him again," a bartender at the Sazerac confided. "It's a wonder he don't leave town. He could go to St. Louis and spend that dough he salted away there."

Jimmie-Behind-the-Stove came in, and Steve beckoned him to a table, bought him a drink. "Have you seen Wilkeson lately?" he asked.

"This week he deals three-card monte at the Plaza Bit."

"What about a guy named Lou Thatcher?"

"He is a bad one, Mr. Mulgrave. Other bad men are with him at the Hangout. Some day they will work up mischief."

"If you get wind of anything, let me know. If you can't find me, leave word with Ricardo Gonzales in his office over the bank." Steve ordered a second drink for Jimmie and then crossed the plaza to Gonzales's office.

176

He found Christine there. They were talking about Ron Garroway. "It might be just the thing for him," the lawyer was saying.

"Did you hear, Steve?" Christine exclaimed. "Ron just rode over to Lynx Creek to look at the Cass Pomeroy place."

"He's taking up," Gonzales added, "right where he left off a year ago."

Steve remembered. Ron Garroway had come to Prescott looking for a small ranch layout where he could start in the livestock business. The Pomeroy place was now deserted and could never be used again by Pomeroy. At the very least the man was due for a long prison term.

"Wish I'd known," Steve brooded. "I'd've ridden to Lynx Creek with him. He's not armed, and he might run into trouble."

Gonzales cocked an eyebrow. "Trouble? Why?"

"It's an empty house off by itself. Any one of a dozen outlaws could be hiding in it. Someone like Ernie Jacks. No telling which way Jacks went after I turned him loose."

But at sunset Ron came back from Lynx Creek unharmed. "It's a neat little place," he reported. "If the price is right, wouldn't mind taking it over. I'd get rid of those horses and stock it with white-face cows."

Steve remembered a Wichita sister named Ruth. Claude Crocker's widow. "Chances are she'll put it on the market someday. She won't want to run it herself. Did you see any sign that somebody's been holing up there?"

"Yes, Steve. Five men have been playing poker on the kitchen table. Deck of cards there and some poker chips. And this." Ron held up a bit check issued by a saloon. Whiskey in Prescott was two drinks for a quarter. When a customer took one drink and laid down a twenty-five-cent piece, the bartender gave him a check worth one bit, or twelve and one-half cents, in change. Later he could use it to buy another whiskey.

Steve saw that this one had been issued by the Hassayampa Hangout. "It's a hole-up they've spotted," he concluded. "The Lou Thatcher gang, probably. Next time you ride over to the Pomeroy place, Ron, better take me along with you."

That was Wednesday. Thursday passed quietly, but on Friday came word from Camp Verde that a sheepherder had been shot dead by a ranch line rider. The killer was known to be fast with a gun, and Roy St. John, senior deputy, decided it might take two to arrest him. "You can ride over there with me, Herbert."

It was a thirty-eight-mile ride to Camp Verde, so they weren't likely to be back before late Monday. It left Steve alone in the sheriff's office with no other lawmen in town except Mel Leonard and a constable who served as night watchman on the plaza.

When Friday night and most of Saturday passed without any serious disturbance, Steve gave a sigh of relief. Late Saturday he saw a buckboard roll into the plaza and stop at Shull's stable. Chad Granby and Alf Sligo got out of it. By the sour look on Granby's face, he hadn't yet found what he'd been searching for at the Skull Valley ranch.

Probably he was in town for the weekend to sign papers, make decisions, and check the bullion output from his mine and smelter. Monday he would haul a load of groceries back to the ranch and carry on with his search there. Steve watched Granby and his bodyguard walk to Goodwin Street and disappear up the steps to Granby's office.

Many others saw Granby's return to town. All of Whiskey Row saw it as well as sidewalk loungers and shoppers on four sides of the plaza. A tall, sullen lawyer saw it from his office window, and half an hour later he crossed Cortez Street to the courthouse. There he found Steve at Joe Walker's desk.

He looked haggard, distraught, even frightened. A front tooth was still missing, and his tailor-made suit lacked its usual meticulous press. "I want protection, Mulgrave," he said.

Steve eyed him curiously. "That's what we're here for, Maxwell. To protect the public. Want to lodge a complaint against someone?"

"All I want is protection," Maxwell said. "Sligo's in town and he'd as lief kill me as not."

"Sligo, huh? Yeh, I just saw him come in. He beat you up once, and you think he'll do it again? Last time he used a club, and this time he might use a gun? If you'll swear out a complaint I'll go pick him up."

"All I want," the lawyer persisted, "is a deputy to stay with me till Sligo leaves town."

It was a reasonable request, and Steve thought it over. "We're short-handed," he said finally. "Look, Maxwell. You go over to the Williams House, take a

179

room, lock your door, and stay there over the weekend. Give me the keys to your office and living quarters. Over Klein's bakeshop, aren't they? Office in front, living rooms in back?"

"That's right." Frank Maxwell laid a ring of keys on the desk.

"Okay," Steve promised. "I'll sit in your office and sleep in your bed till Monday morning. If Sligo comes pussyfooting in, he'll find me instead of you."

Maxwell left him and Steve looked up two people: Mel Leonard and Ricardo Gonzales. He told them, and no one else, where he could be found till Monday morning.

CHAPTER
SEVENTEEN

As dark came to the plaza that Saturday night, Steve stopped in at the Williams House to look at the book. The last registration was Frank Maxwell's. From there he went up to the Cortez Street side of the plaza until he came to a bakeshop. It was closed for the night, as were the stores on either side of it.

Making sure no one saw him, he hurried up the steps which led to Maxwell's office and living quarters. An upper hallway had an oil lamp in a wall bracket, and he lighted it. There were two doors: one at the front of the hall giving to a law office, another at the back giving to a bachelor apartment.

Steve unlocked both doors. The office had two windows looking out on the plaza, and he pulled down both shades. Then he lighted a lamp and placed it so that a glow on the shades would tell anyone looking up from the street that the office was occupied.

He did the same in the bedroom of the living quarters at the rear. This room had a window giving on an alley, and an inner door giving on a kitchen. With the shades drawn and the bedroom lighted, the quarters would seem to be occupied. The kitchen had a rear door to a porch from which steps led down to the

181

alley. Steve left that door unlocked. If Sligo came calling tonight, he wouldn't need to crash in or pick locks.

In the front office Steve sat down at Maxwell's big flat-top desk. He took the gun from his holster and laid it on the desk. The office had a table, a filing cabinet, a leather chair for clients. It would be a long, tedious wait, and maybe Sligo wouldn't come at all. Presently Steve went to a window and shifted the shade a few inches to look out on the plaza. The far side of it, Whiskey Row, showed door glows from eight saloons. The sidewalk over there was milling with miners, cowboys, drifters. On the Gurley Street side there were only two saloon lights and another from the Williams House lobby. Bashford's big store was dark. On the Goodwin Street side Steve could see only a few street-level lights and one dim window light over the general offices of the Skyline company. It meant that Chad Granby was at his desk, signing papers and answering accumulated mail. Alf Sligo would be with him. Over the years Chad Granby had foreclosed many mortgages, squeezed many debtors, overworked and underpaid many employees. Any one of them could be a threat to him.

This side of the plaza, Cortez Street, was darkest of all. Mainly it had Sol Lewis's bank and the three big general stores — Buffum's, Head's, and Goldwater's. All of them were dark. Hitchrails on this side were empty. Across on Whiskey Row, every hitchrail was lined with horses.

182

He went back to Maxwell's desk to see what he could find there. The drawers were locked, and so was the filing cabinet. A basket of incoming mail showed only one letter. It was from the Gilmer, Salisbury's & Company stage line and in polite terms announced that Frank Maxwell's services as attorney were no longer required.

Many such notices must have come in this past week. So why didn't Maxwell close up and leave town? Perhaps he planned to do so but didn't want his retreat to seem too hurried, lest it be taken for the panic of guilt. A recent copy of the St. Louis *Post-Dispatch* lay on the table. It must have come by mail — and Steve could see a reason for it. Maxwell had $23,000 in a St. Louis savings account, and only by going to St. Louis in person could he withdraw it. Yet he'd be cautious about doing that. Maybe the law at St. Louis was waiting for him, ready to accuse him of bribing the thief Jerome Lambert. Or he might be afraid that Chad Granby, through a St. Louis attorney, had filed suit for recovery and had impounded the savings account pending a court's judgment.

In any such case the St. Louis newspaper should mention it. Which could be why Maxwell had sent for current copies of the *Post-Dispatch*.

So the lawyer was standing pat here, Steve concluded, until he was sure the coast was clear at St. Louis. Then he could slip quietly and forever out of Arizona.

In the St. Louis paper Steve found a follow-up story on the treachery and suicide of Lambert, but there was

183

no mention of Maxwell. Nothing, after all, could be proved against Maxwell. Lambert had told no tale on him.

For the next several hours Steve sat at the desk with his gun within reach, ready for a visit from Sligo. No one came. The man might never come. The one beating he'd given Maxwell might be considered enough. Whatever he did would be on orders from Granby. Quite likely Granby had set a deadline, a date by which Maxwell must return the $24,000 "or else." The "else" would be dealt him by Sligo.

Tonight Sligo would conclude from the glow at this front window that Maxwell was in his office. Would he walk into the trap?

When by midnight he hadn't, Steve blew out the lamp and went back to the living quarters. He laid his gun on the bed, leaving the hallway door unlocked, inviting Sligo. He sat on the bed for another hour in the dark. No ascending boot made a creak on the stairs. No door squeaked open. At half past one he decided Sligo wasn't coming. He locked the apartment doors and went to bed. Just before he fell asleep he heard a patter of rain against the window.

In midmorning he wakened and made breakfast. The kitchen offered coffee, bacon, and bread. It was still raining gently outside.

Going forward to the law office, he planned to spend a silent day there, watching from its window for sign of Granby or Sligo. Then he saw a spot of fresh mud. It was on the floor just inside the office door. It meant

184

there'd been an after-midnight intrusion. Sligo, after all, had come slipping in to deal with Maxwell.

Today was Sunday. Would he come again tonight?

All that dreary day Steve watched cautiously from a window. Just after midday the rain stopped. Again, only the Whiskey Row side of the plaza was busy. Ranch and mine men in for the weekend gave a brisk trade to the bars and games over there.

The afternoon dragged tediously. The plaza showed no sign of Granby, Sligo, or Frank Maxwell. Steve saw Ron and Christine stroll down Gurley and go into George Kendall's drugstore. Ron was probably treating her to ice cream or soda water. When they reappeared they crossed over to the courthouse basement. *Looking for me*, Steve concluded. It meant that Gonzales had kept the secret of his stake-out here at Maxwell's office.

Steve's gaze followed wistfully as Ron walked Christine back toward Marina Street. It looked like Ron had the inside track there. Emily Wardell had chided him about it. "Don't let him beat your time, Steve," she'd warned. He had a feeling that Emily was on his side.

At sundown he saw one of Granby's clerks go into the Bashford store. Bashford kept his grocery department open on Sundays for the benefit of countrymen who couldn't come in during the week. The clerk came out with a bulging sack, followed by Bashford's delivery man with a similar sack. The two walked to the Shull stable, went in, and came out empty-handed.

185

It meant that Granby had given the clerk a list of food supplies needed at the Skull Valley ranch. They were now stowed in Granby's rig so that he and Sligo could get an early start Monday morning.

In the kitchen Steve made supper, and when he finished eating, it was dark. Again he lighted a hall lamp, an office lamp, and a bedroom lamp. Again he sat in the office waiting for Sligo.

After a few hours he caught himself napping. For a minute he'd been at the mercy of Sligo. It mustn't happen again. He opened the office door a few inches, then took a heavy law book and balanced it on top of the door. Anyone pushing the door open would cause the book to fall, and the thump should warn him in time.

But again midnight came without bringing Sligo. Soon after that he blew out the office lamp, leaving the hallway lamp burning. If the bedroom door was opened, enough indirect light would filter in to let Sligo see the shape of a sleeper in bed.

He fashioned the shape with a bolster, pillows, and a roll of blankets. In the dimness Frank Maxwell would seem to be where he should be after midnight, asleep in his own bed.

Tonight he left the bedroom door closed but unlocked. He went into the dark kitchen and sat with a gun on his knees. He might as well play the game out, even if it took till daylight. Soon after daybreak Sligo was due to drive Granby back to Skull Valley.

Again he caught himself drowsing. He lighted a candle, heated coffee, and drank two cups. It was three a.m. He blew out the candle and sat down again to wait for Sligo.

A creaking sound on the stairs warned him. Someone was coming stealthily up. Footsteps crossing the hall were catlike, barely audible. A door opened, but it wasn't the bedroom. Sligo was first checking the office.

Minutes later Steve heard the bedroom doorknob turn. As the door opened, a dim glow came in from the hallway. Steve stood up, gun in hand. He was in the dark kitchen just inside the open doorway to the bedroom.

A stealthy step advanced toward the bed, and in a moment Steve made out the silhouette of Sligo. He wasn't aiming his gun, but was clubbing it for a blow. The roar of a shot would give an alarm; so the man clearly meant not to shoot Maxwell but to pistol-whip him. He could leave Maxwell dead or nearly dead and slip quietly away.

Steve let him get to the bedside and raise his gun to strike. Then, "That's far enough, Sligo."

The man whirled, shooting. He was shooting into darkness because the kitchen was unlighted, and the bedroom itself had only indirect light from the hall. Even then a bullet scratched Steve's cheek and left a red line there. Steve squeezed his own trigger twice, shooting to cripple but not to kill. A bullet to each arm above the elbow.

Alf Sligo dropped his gun, and his yell might have been heard halfway across the plaza. He went to his knees with two smashed arm-bones, his screams fading into sobs of pain. "I'll get you a doctor," Steve promised quietly, and picked up the man's gun.

He went forward to the law office, opened a window, took a police whistle from his pocket, and blew it. A night watchman, Mel Leonard's assistant, should be patrolling the plaza.

When the watchman answered, Steve called him up to the office. "Sligo," he reported, "slipped in gunning for Maxwell. I had to drop him. Put him on the bed and then watch him while I fetch Doctor Day."

In the morning a hearing was held at the courthouse. Judge Carttier and District Attorney Ferd Oliver had already listened to Sligo's story at the hospital, where he'd been for the past several hours. Maxwell owed him money, the man said. He'd gone up there to collect. Chad Granby, knew nothing about it. That was his story and he stuck to it.

Granby didn't even appear. But the loss of his bodyguard delayed his return to Skull Valley. He'd need to get himself another one, and all of Whiskey Row wondered who it would be.

By midafternoon of Monday Whiskey Row had the answer. A messenger left the Skyline offices and was seen going into the Plaza Bit saloon. When the messenger reappeared, he had Three-Card Wilkeson in tow. And early Tuesday morning when the Granby buckboard rolled westerly out of town, the swarthy, gunslung man who held the reins was Wilkeson.

"Not a bad trade," Mel Leonard remarked to Steve Mulgrave. "He can shoot just as straight, and he's a heap smarter than Sligo."

188

Steve crossed to the Williams House and found Frank Maxwell in his room there. "You can go home now, Maxie," he said, tossing him a ring of keys.

CHAPTER
EIGHTEEN

A westbound Southern Pacific train, three sweltering hours out of Tucson, whistled for its next stop. A brakeman came through the coach, shouting: "All out for Maricopa! Stage connection for Wickenburg and Prescott."

The cars rattled over switchpoints and came to a stop at a brand new frame depot. Only for the last few weeks had the Southern Pacific been completed all the way from El Paso to San Francisco.

Sheriff Joe Walker, with a haggard prisoner handcuffed to his left wrist, was the last passenger to disembark. Some would change here for stage points north, mainly for Wickenburg and Prescott. "You've behaved pretty well so far, Cass," Walker said. "Don't start giving me any trouble now."

"How long," Pomeroy muttered, "will we be on that damned stage?"

"Close to forty hours. No use grousing about it. It's as hard on me as it is on you."

The Concord coach for Prescott was waiting just beyond the depot. Joe Walker had telegraphed ahead for tickets and so was sure of seats. The depot platform was crowded. Some were getting on the train for passage to

Gila Bend, Yuma, or points in California. The sheriff of Yavapai County, awkwardly pushing through the crowd with his prisoner, came to a startled halt when he recognized one of those who were boarding the westbound train.

"Hell's bells! Wonder where *he's* going!"

Harley Rood of Wickenburg, with a heavy suitcase in hand, quickly boarded a sleeping car and was out of Walker's sight. The sheriff's first impulse was to challenge and stop him. But after a moment's thought he knew he couldn't. He was already encumbered with a prisoner. And there was no solid case against Rood. Nothing more than a loose theory that he'd conspired with Granby and Pendleton nine years ago to defraud Adam Mayberry.

I can at least find out where he's going, Walker concluded. He went into the railroad depot, dragging his prisoner with him. The Maricopa agent, whom he knew quite well, was at the ticket window. "Look, Dave, Harley Rood just bought a ticket for somewhere west of here. How far's he going?"

"All the way to Frisco, Joe. Sleeping-car passage all the way through."

"Did he buy a round-trip ticket?"

"Nope. Only a one-way ticket. Why? Is he wanted for something?"

"Nothing I can hold him for. Thanks, Dave."

The train for California pulled out. And a few minutes later Joe Walker, still linked to Cass Pomeroy, boarded a north-bound stagecoach for Wickenburg and Prescott.

191

After two nights and a day of weary travel, they were met at the Prescott stage station by Roy St. John and Steve Mulgrave.

The sheriff, sleepy-eyed and road-weary, was glad to turn Pomeroy over to them. "He's all yours, Roy." He unlocked a steel link and transferred it to the wrist of St. John. "I should've sent one of your boys after him. Next time I will."

"Any trouble on the way?" St. John asked him.

"Nothing, except I bumped into Harley Rood at Maricopa. He was climbing on an S.P. train for Frisco."

"Making a run for it?" Steve suggested.

"Looks like it. During the meal stop at Wickenburg I asked a few questions. They say he closed his shop there and drew his money out of the bank. Last we'll see of him, likely. What's been going on around here?"

"Sligo," Roy St. John reported with a grin, "went after Frank Maxwell again. Didn't get very far, though. Steve here'll tell you about it. It was his party. I'd better shag Pomeroy to his cell. Come along, Cass."

Pomeroy, with a haggard, fearful look at a courtyard where only last fall two of his friends had been hanged, for a moment pulled back with all his despairing strength, then followed reluctantly along.

"His sister Ruth from Wichita," Steve told the sheriff, "just got here. She's retaining Tom Rush to defend him." He picked up the sheriff's satchel. "I'll tote this to your office."

"I'll get something to eat first, Steve. Haven't had a decent meal since I left Tucson."

The eating place Walker decided on was Wan Sung's restaurant on Granite Street. In addition to his fan-tan dive and joss house, Wan Sung served the best chop suey and egg noodles in northern Arizona.

This morning he served them in person. "Now give me the lowdown on Sligo," Walker prompted.

Steve told him about the weekend stake-out. "With two busted arms Sligo won't be using a gun for the next couple of months. Chad Granby, you understand, won't admit having anything to do with it."

"Chad's still out at the Skull Valley ranch?"

Steve nodded. "Hunting for something planted there nine years ago by Rood, we think. Nothing we can do about it. He owns the place and what he does there's his business. He's got a new bodyguard now. Guess who."

"They told me about it," the sheriff said, "at the Skull Valley stage stop. Three-Card Wilkeson."

"Granby's got everybody guessing, Sheriff, as to what he's up to. You ought to hear the talk along Whiskey Row. You can pick up a dozen theories about why he bought the ranch and moved out there."

"What about Frank Maxwell?"

"The bets are he'll pull out of here one of these days. Might as well. His law practice is all shot to pieces. Nobody trusts him anymore. Only kind of customer he can get nowadays is some barroom brawler like that bunch down at the Hassayampa Hangout."

At that same moment, in Judge Carttier's court, Maxwell was representing such a client, Lou Thatcher

193

stood before the bench charged with disorderly conduct at one of the Granite Street bagnios. Attorney Maxwell stood beside him. He offered the only defense possible that the complaining witness herself was a woman of low character and not to be trusted.

"The fine," Judge Carttier decreed, "will be twenty-five dollars. Next case."

Paying the fine took all of Thatcher's pocket money. "How much do I owe you?" he asked Maxwell.

"Twenty dollars. Bring it to my office." Abruptly Maxwell left the courtroom and went to his quarters over Klein's bakeshop. It was a bitter, humiliating experience, being reduced to representing only the Prescott underworld.

The morning mail was on his desk, and among it was another issue of the St. Louis *Post-Dispatch*. Maxwell skimmed through it, relieved to find no further mention of the Lambert case. As soon as he was sure the coast was clear at St. Louis, he'd head there by stage and train, pick up his stake, and start fresh somewhere else.

But there was something he wanted to do first. It had gnawed on him day and night since he'd been fired by Granby, and especially since he'd been beaten up by Granby's man Sligo. Sligo's latest attack, although foiled by Steve Mulgrave, had only added to the bitterness — and to a compulsion for getting even. Right now more than anything else he wanted revenge on Chad Granby.

Was there a way to get it, without risk to himself, before he left Prescott?

What was Granby up to these days — spending most of his time on an unstocked cattle ranch a five-hour drive west of town? The man was a millionaire mine operator, money lender, and opportunist promoter. He might buy a block of improved land as an investment, but it was quite out of his character to live on it. Was Granby in trouble of some kind? Was some shady dealing of his past about to catch up with him?

Like many others in Prescott, Maxwell hadn't failed to notice a certain nervous caution in Chad Granby ever since the daughter of a man who'd mysteriously disappeared nine years ago had arrived here. Not till then had Maxwell learned that the disappearance had probably occurred on a ridge above Milk Creek — the very location of Granby's Skyline bonanza. An area in which Steve Mulgrave had found the bullet-punctured skull of a horse and a hint that the rider of that horse had arrived in Arizona nine years ago on the steamship *Newbern*.

Whiskey Row was rife with rumors as to what the connection could be. Maxwell had heard them all and believed none of them. He did know that a Wickenburg assayer had been mentioned in connection with the mystery, and that Granby had made a quick round trip to Wickenburg recently, soon after which the assayer had closed shop and left the territory.

The lawyer was puzzling over this when he heard bootsteps coming up from the street. The office door opened and his most recent client came in. "Here's what I owe you, lawyer man." The Hassayampa Hangout gang leader, Lou Thatcher, dropped twenty dollars on the desk.

Prompt payment of the fee didn't surprise Maxwell. An outlaw like Thatcher might need a lawyer at any moment, and so would keep in good standing with one who'd already served him. No doubt this man had a trail of crime back of him, and right now he was probably on the lookout for an opportunity to make another clean-up of some kind — perhaps a bullion shipment by stage or train, or maybe a fat payroll. The inside word was that he'd organized a five-man crew down at the Hangout and was waiting there, like a spider in a web, for just the right chance.

Why not throw him a chance? As Thatcher was about to leave the office, the vague outline of an idea came to Maxwell. "What's your hurry?" he invited. "Sit down and have a drink."

Thatcher, wearing a gunless gunbelt, eyed him cautiously and then sat down. Maxwell took whiskey from his desk and poured two glasses.

"Ever hear of Chad Granby?"

"Yeh. What about him?"

The lawyer lowered his voice. "I was just thinking you might get a job with him."

"A job?" Thatcher's lip curved with contempt. "What would I want with a job?" In his world, jobs were for suckers.

Maxwell reassured him. "This would be a job sort of in your line. A gun job. I mean a bodyguard job."

Thatcher still didn't show any interest. "They tell me he's already got a bodyguard. Took on a guy named Wilkeson."

196

"That's right," Maxwell agreed. "But he's likely to need more than one guard any day now. Him out there at that lonely ranch sitting on all that cash."

The word cash made a difference. Thatcher's eyes narrowed and his ears sharpened. "Yeh? I don't getcha. What's he doin' out there anyway?"

The lawyer leaned across the desk with his voice still lower. "He's playing safe, Thatcher, in case the roof falls in on him right suddenly. Maybe it won't, but he's playing it safe just in case. You heard about that girl from Ohio?"

"I hear bar talk," Thatcher said. "You never know how much of it to believe. They say you usta be lawyer for that guy, so you oughta know. What's the lowdown?"

"Nobody knows for sure," the lawyer admitted, "but chances are he stole that bonanza of his from the girl's father and they're about to get the goods on him. It's got a murder smell to it, and if they can prove it, Granby'll need to make fast tracks for the coast. With as much hard cash as he can lay hands on. One thing I do know. He's been cashing in his local investments and drawing his money out of the Prescott bank."

Lou Thatcher listened, his mouth hanging open. "You tryin' to tell me he's got it all out there at that Skull Valley ranch?"

"All he can lay hands on," Maxwell insisted. "Came in last weekend just to pick up some more. That's why I say he needs more than one bodyguard. Wilkeson's pretty handy with a gun, all right, but he wouldn't be much good against a five-man raid."

"It don't make sense," Thatcher argued after weighing the probabilities. "That guy wouldn't run out and leave a million-dollar mine behind him."

"He would if they could prove murder guilt on him. That Skyline property won't do him any good after they hang him. One of the other men in on it, a Wickenburg Assayer, has already high-tailed for the coast."

The point scored with Thatcher. News traveled fast along Whiskey Row, and it was already widely known that Harley Rood had left suddenly and permanently for San Francisco. It seemed to support Maxwell's information about Granby and brought a greedy glint to Thatcher's eyes.

The lawyer drove his argument home. "Skull Valley," he reminded his client, "is two stage stations closer to the coast than Prescott. Five hours by stage or saddle. If he has to do a fast fade-out, it'll give him just that much of a jump on the sheriff."

Thatcher downed the last of his whiskey. "How much dough," he asked avidly, "do you reckon he's got out there?"

The attorney shrugged. "No telling. Not less than a hundred thousand, I'd say. Probably got another hundred thousand or so salted away in a Frisco bank. Anyway he ought to have more than one bodyguard. Might be a chance for you to get on."

Lou Thatcher wiped his lips and stood up. "Maybe you're right," he said carelessly as he moved toward the door. "I'll think it over."

Maxwell heard him clump down the steps to the Cortez Street walk. From his window he watched the man hurry across the plaza, heading west along Gurley toward the Hassayampa Hangout. He'd lose no time in confiding to his coterie of heelers there.

One thing was certain. A day-pay bodyguard job wouldn't interest Thatcher. But a bagful of money would. Easy pickings — with only Wilkeson to guard it. Granby himself didn't count. Only one gun would stand between Granby and a quintet of Hassayampa Hangout raiders.

For Maxwell it would be sweet revenge. The raid would be a blind haul, of course. They'd find nothing but pocket money on Granby. But after assaulting him and gunning down Wilkeson, they'd hardly dare to leave Granby alive.

All without in any way implicating Maxwell. He hadn't advised or suggested a raid. He'd merely tipped a client as to where he might get a day-pay job. All perfectly legal and ethical.

Frank Maxwell poured himself another drink. He'd stay in Prescott until news of the raid at Skull Valley came in. Then, after savoring his revenge, he'd head for St. Louis. The Thatcher gang wouldn't be likely to wait long. A twenty-six-mile night ride and a blast of gunfire — and whatever Granby planned to get away with would be theirs.

CHAPTER
NINETEEN

Ron Garroway was still asleep in the backyard bunk cabin when Steve made his own breakfast and then hurried to the office of Ricardo Gonzales. It was to be another strategy conference in the campaign to advance the interests of Christine Mayberry.

The lawyer showed disappointment when Steve walked in alone. "I thought Ron and Christine would come with you, Estevan."

"They're not up yet," Steve reported with a grimace. "He drove her out to look at a ranch yesterday, and they didn't get back till after dark."

"The Pomeroy ranch on Lynx Creek?"

"Not that one. John Lee's American ranch nine miles northwest ot town. There's a For Sale ad on it in the *Miner.*"

"I have heard," Gonzales murmured, "that it is the best small ranch in Yavapai County." Slyly he added, "It would make a lovely home for them, Estevan."

Steve abruptly changed the subject. "Speaking of ranches, Lem Hopper's gone to Bill Becker's Stirrup layout in Lonesome Valley, where he's got a job breaking broncos. Shorty Brill went with him to see if he can get on himself. Says he doesn't want to sponge any longer on Mrs. Wardell."

"What about Sheriff Walker's staff?" Gonzales asked.

"Millard's back from Gilette. St. John and Herbert just brought a prisoner back from Camp Verde. So the sheriff's got his full force now except for Kim Long, who's still patrolling the railroad camps."

"And you?"

"I've still got my badge. Asked Walker to let me take another ride out to Granby. I found a horse skull and a slicker that other time; maybe I could pick up something else."

"And what does the sheriff say?"

"Told me to wait a few days longer till we find out what Granby's up to out at the Skull Valley ranch, or if he finds what he's looking for. Walker's got a hunch that something's about to break loose out there."

"I too have such a feeling, Estevan. He will either find a message planted by Harley Rood, or he will fail to find it. If he finds it he will destroy it and be safe. Rood himself has left the territory and will worry him no more. If he does not find it he will conclude it was never there; so he will post a caretaker to keep away trespassers, then return to his affairs in town."

"And where," Steve wondered, "would that leave Christine Mayberry?"

"With nothing she can take to court," Gonzales conceded sadly. "Even if we could prove that Isaac Pendleton shot her father and jumped his claim, we still could not prove whether or not Granby connived with him. Granby would deny it, saying that a prospector

201

he'd grubstaked had filed a claim and that he'd merely accepted the fifty-percent share due him. With Rood gone and Pendleton dead, we'd have nothing left but a bagful of suspicions."

"Then we've been wasting our time!" Steve fretted.

The attorney gave a Latin shrug. "Who can say? Strange things have happened in this matter. Who knows what will happen next?" He looked at Steve's discouraged face and smiled. "Not only in affairs of property, but in the other affair which troubles you, my friend. You think you have lost her, do you not? That she has love for Ronaldo? That she goes to look at a ranch with him because they may some day live there? But perhaps it is only because she has been sorry for him — this pleasant young man who has been unjustly accused, hiding from the hangman for a year and then, when he returns to give himself up, beaten nearly to death by ruffians . . . so she feels pity for him and does not say no when he asks her to drive into the country and return by moonlight . . . And you, what do you do, Estevan? Have you asked her for a date? Do you make love? You do not even buy her a soda water at the drugstore. Even Frank Maxwell asks her to a theater show. Only you are the laggard —"

He stopped suddenly when he heard footsteps coming up to this office floor. "Perhaps here she comes now," he suggested. "Or maybe it is Ronaldo."

The knock was timid, and they knew it couldn't be either Ron or Christine. "Enter," Gonzales invited.

The entrance was as timid as the knock. It was a person Steve had never seen anywhere except on

Whiskey Row. This east side of the plaza had rarely if ever been visited by Jimmie-Behind-the-Stove.

"I inquired at Mrs. Wardell's," he said. "She told me I could find you here."

"You're onto something?" Steve prompted.

"Perhaps," the saloon derelict answered. "Last night I was in the Palace bar when Frenchy LaRue came in. He had just been at the Hassayampa Hangout — a place I do not go myself. Frenchy thinks that Lou Thatcher and four others are riding to hold up a stagecoach; perhaps the Wickenburg stage, perhaps the Gilette stage, or maybe the one which goes to Flagstaff and Canyon Diablo."

"Yeh? What gave Frenchy an idea like that?"

"Because one of the men tied five saddled horses at the Hangout hitchrail. He came in and whispered to Thatcher and the others. Thatcher spoke to the bartender, who handed them their five guns."

"Makes sense," Steve agreed shrewdly. "They'd have their guns checked at the bar to keep from getting fined. Went out and rode away, did they?"

"Yes, sir," Jimmie confirmed. "But as they went out Frenchy LaRue heard one of them say to Thatcher, 'Are you sure the old man's got only one bodyguard?' And Thatcher said, 'Dead sure of it; let's ride.' Then they went out and rode away."

"Which direction?"

"West on Gurley Street, toward Thumb Butte."

"Thanks, Jimmie. Here's something to celebrate with." Steve gave the remittance of a five-dollar bill.

"Only one way to figure it, Rick," Steve said when the man left them. "For some reason they think Chad Granby's got a wad of dough on him. And nobody with him but Wilkeson."

"You must hurry, Estevan," Gonzales advised, "and tell the sheriff."

Steve lost no time doing it. He found Joe Walker in the basement office with three of his deputies. Millard, boots propped on a desk, was twirling a cigarette. St. John and Herbert, back yesterday from Camp Verde, looked relaxed after a night's rest. The full staff was there with the exception of Kim Long.

"What's up?" Walker asked as Steve burst in on them.

"The devil's up. A raid on Chad Granby." Quickly Steve relayed the information given him by Jimmie-Behind-the-Stove.

Only Millard was inclined to discount it. "Why," he argued, "would Granby have a lot of money out there?"

"Makes no difference whether he has or not," Steve countered. "Point is that Thatcher *thinks* he's got something worth cracking down on. There's a flock of theories floating around town about why Granby's out there, and Thatcher could believe any one of them. It's twenty-six miles to Skull Valley, and he wouldn't ride that far just for small change. Remember what one of 'em said: 'You sure the old man's only got one bodyguard?' Who else could he mean but Granby and Wilkeson?"

Sheriff Walker smacked his fist into his palm. "You're right, Steve; it doesn't fit anyone but Granby and

204

Wilkeson. Anyway it clears two decks for us. We've been looking for a legitimate excuse to barge in on Granby and find out what he's doing there. Now we've got it. And we've been trying to get something on the Hangout gang. Now we've got it. We follow 'em to the ranch, gun it out with 'em if they're bothering Granby; if they're not, we tell Granby we just rode out there to protect him from raiders. Go saddle up five mounts, Roy. There's five of those Hangouters, and we'd better match 'em gun for gun."

It was still only half past ten when Joe Walker and four of his deputies rode out West Gurley Street and took a trail which led just north of Thumb Butte. Morning sunlight shone brightly on the pine trees. Each saddle scabbard had a carbine, and each belt had a holstered forty-five.

"Only thing I don't like about this fight," St. John complained, "is that we'll be on the same side with Three-Card Wilkeson."

Millard was still dubious. "Even if the Hangouters went there," he argued, "we'll be too late. They made a night ride and must've got there by daybreak. They'll have done their dirt and be gone by now."

"All the more reason to hurry," Walker said. He spurred to a lope.

The route they were riding would be three miles shorter than the stage road, which hooked north via Iron Springs. "We can make it by midafternoon," St. John calculated.

"On winded horses," Millard muttered. "We'd need fresh ones to chase Thatcher."

A rise toward the north shoulder of Thumb Butte slowed them to a walk. Soon they skirted the high, slender peak which was like a giant thumb pointing to the sky. Beyond, they were in the pine country, passing by a sawmill. The Sierra Prietas rose to the left, forcing them to veer right toward the head of Iron Springs Wash.

An hour's ride from town brought them to Willow Creek near its head. They splashed across its shallow trickle, coming out in an open basin to the north of Sugarloaf Mountain. Steve knew the route well; it was a shortcut he'd often used riding to Prescott from the Wardell ranch.

"Those Hangouters didn't come this way," Millard said.

"Don't see any fresh tracks."

"Lots of ways they could've gone," Herbert said. "Might even've took the stage road. At night nobody'd see 'em."

Noon found them on the south fork of Iron Springs Wash, where there was a seep of water. Walker ordered a short rest to let the mounts blow. "Millard's right," he admitted. "We're fourteen hours behind Thatcher. He could do his work on Granby and be long gone by now."

"I look to find two dead men," Millard persisted. "Wilkeson and Granby."

The next wash they hit was an upper fork of Skull Valley Creek. From here it would be a water grade all the way to the ranch. Riding single file, the posse followed down the wash. It was soft sand and the

206

absence of tracks made it certain that Thatcher's crew had taken some other route.

"Unless," Herbert said, "that moocher Englishman gave us a bum steer. He passed it on secondhand from Frenchy LaRue."

Steve had to admit it was a secondhand tip. When they struck the main fork of Skull Valley Creek and came in sight of the ranch buildings, everything looked peaceful and undisturbed. The east fence of the ranch had a creek-bank gate, and they passed through it. Now they were in a hay meadow. Another half-mile and they could see two loose horses in the ranch corral. That would be Granby's buckboard team. The buckboard itself stood in front of the barn. Everything seemed as it should be. Yes, a secondhand tip could have been garbled in some way. Maybe the five Hangouters had ridden off to rob a stagecoach, or a mine payroll somewhere in the Bradshaws.

The posse loped into the barnyard and reined up in front of the house. The chimney showed no smoke. "Anybody home?" Walker shouted.

No one answered. "Maybe," St. John suggested, "they went to the station. It was only two miles from here."

Walker shook his head. "How would they get there, Roy?" He thumbed toward the corraled buckboard team. "It's a cinch they wouldn't walk." He dismounted and went to the house door. The four deputies followed, spurs clanking.

A knock brought no answer from Granby or Wilkeson. The sheriff tried the door, found it unlocked, pushed it open.

The parlor was empty, but one look told Steve that raiders had been there. Pulled-out drawers and gutted cushions meant that the room had been violently searched. Then a feeble moan came from a room beyond.

On the floor there they found a bloody Chad Granby with barely a breath of life left in him. He hadn't been shot, but he was battered and bruised and two ribs had been kicked in. The guard he'd hired to defend him was nowhere in the house.

The floor and grounds showed no empty shells, no evidence of a gunfight. "When Wilkie saw 'em coming," Herbert guessed, "he likely joined the Hangouters. Rode off with 'em with whatever they picked up here. He's their kind, anyway."

"More likely," St. John thought, "he's down in the barn with a skinful of slugs."

"See if you can find him," Walker ordered. "Steve, let's see if we can get something out of Granby."

In the kitchen Steve found a pint of brandy. They put Granby on a bed and held the liquor to his lips. "Who did it?" Joe Walker kept repeating the question.

After a patient while he got a word out of Granby. "Five of them," the man whispered, "They called him Thatch . . ."

Millard came in from the outsheds to report that they'd failed to find the bodyguard Wilkeson, dead or alive.

"Hitch up the buckboard team," Walker directed, "Only chance to save Granby's life is to get him to the Prescott hospital. Take out the back seat and put a mattress in the wagon bed. You or Herbert can haul him to town. Be as easy as you can on him."

Millard went out, and a minute later Steve saw Granby moving his lips. "He wants to tell us something, Sheriff."

Walker leaned over him. "What is it, Mr. Granby? Why did they raid you?"

The bruised man lay there, pale as death, until Steve again held brandy to his lips. Then with an effort Chad Granby managed his first clear statement. "Thought I had money here; told 'em I didn't; wouldn't believe me . . ."

"So they beat you up," Walker coaxed, "What made them think you had money here?"

This brought no response. Instead Steve heard the name Wilkeson. It was spoken bitterly.

"Wilkeson? Yes, what about him?"

"He deserted me," Granby told them. "Saw 'em coming and sneaked out the back way . . ."

That was the last they could get out of Chad Granby. Steve and Joe Walker exchanged grim nods. It would be like Wilkeson. When he saw five outlaws ride up in front, guns out, he could slip away by the back door and get in the creek willows.

"But he'd be afoot," Walker puzzled. "Nothing in the corral but two harness horses."

"He could walk two miles to the Skull Valley stage station," Steve concluded, "and rent a mount there. By now he could be back in Prescott breasting a Whiskey Row bar. And those five Hangouters —"

Steve broke off suddenly, staring at something on the wall, something which instantly trapped his entire attention. Walker saw an oddly alert look form on his face. "You onto somethin', Steve?"

"This room we're in," Steve told him, "was the ranch house guest room. I know because I was foreman here for a long time."

"So what?"

"So it's the room Harley Rood slept in nine years ago, on his way to Wickenburg. It's the room he was in when he wrote the deadwood on Chad Granby and hid it somewhere."

"What of it? Granby's been here a couple of weeks looking for it. He didn't find it, or he wouldn't still be here."

"He'd look everywhere," Steve agreed, "like in the hollow bedposts of that iron bed. But he was too late to look one other place, Sheriff."

The man who'd been foreman here pointed to a faded rectangle, about ten by sixteen inches, on the plaster wall of the room. "For years a framed photograph hung there. That's why the wall behind it faded a little. It was a picture of Henry Wardell. Emily was mighty proud of it. When she put the place up for sale, furniture and all, she held out a few family personals like that framed picture of her husband. It's hanging on her parlor wall right now, at the Marina Street town house."

Walker's eyes widened as he caught Steve's drift. "So maybe Harley Rood —"

210

"Where else," Steve broke in, "could he find a better place to hide his sheet of paper? He could slip it in between the photograph and the frame's backing. If he did, it's still there, after nine years."

"Buckboard's ready," Herbert reported from the doorway. "Mattress and all. We'd better take the stage road, hadn't we?"

Steve and the sheriff, still looking at a faded space on the wall, barely heard him.

CHAPTER
TWENTY

At exactly midnight, Joe Walker and three of his crew rode east from the Skull Valley stage station, taking the regular coach route toward Prescott. They were on fresh mounts and had had five hours' sleep at the station. Deputy Millard had been left at the station with Granby. The station man and his wife had helped him put the man to bed. In the morning Millard would put him on the buckboard mattress and head for the Prescott hospital.

"Ten to one he won't get there alive," Walker said. "But nothing else we can do." There was no doctor nearer than Prescott.

"A younger man might pull through," St. John thought. "But not Granby. He's tough — but not tough enough to survive a mauling like that and two busted ribs."

"One good thing," Herbert put in. "If he don't make it we'll have a murder count against Lou Thatcher."

A hot supper at the Skull Valley station and the five hours' sleep had left them in fair shape for the ride. It would be a bit farther this time because the stage road curved north by way of Iron Springs. They made the

Irons Springs station by three o'clock and had to waken the agent there.

Walker tried to get fresh mounts, but the place had no saddle stock. He settled for coffee for his crew, with grain and a thirty-minute rest for the mounts.

"We'll stop first at the Hangout," he decided as the posse rode on. "The joint stays open all night. Not much chance of finding Thatcher there at daybreak, but it won't hurt to look."

"He probably left Granby for dead," Steve said. "Anyway he'd be leery about showing his face in town."

"Why not?" St. John argued. "He won't know that Granby told tales on him. And it's a cinch Wilkeson won't, because Wilkie don't want people to know he skinned out."

Thumb Butte was in sight when pink dawn began showing beyond the Mogollons. Half an hour later they hit the west end of Gurley Street and cantered down a grade to the wooden bridge across Granite Creek. A block beyond the bridge they drew up in front of the Hassayampa Hangout. At this hour the place was quiet, and when Walker looked in he saw only three customers at the bar.

None of them wore a cartridge belt or seemed likely to be one of the Thatcher gang. "Lou Thatcher been in?" Walker asked the barman.

"Ain't seen him since day before yesterday, Sheriff."

It was probably true. "He'll lie low somewhere," Herbert guessed, "till he finds out if there's any heat on."

It gave Steve an idea. "Look, Sheriff. Not long ago Ron Garroway found sign that those fellas have picked themselves a hide-out." He told about a poker game in a deserted ranch house on Lynx Creek, with a Hassayampa Hangout bar check on the table.

Walker was impressed. "A good place for 'em to hide out," he agreed. "Only five miles from here. Tell you what. We'll leave our horses at Shull's barn to be rubbed down and grained. Everybody get himself some breakfast. In an hour we'll all meet at Shull's and hit the trail for Lynx Creek."

When Steve got to the backyard bunk cabin on Marina Street, he found Ron Garroway up and frying bacon. "Put some on for me, Ron, and pour me some coffee. I need nourishment; I've ridden fifty-six miles and have got five more to go."

"Where to, Steve?"

"Pomeroy's place on Lynx Creek." Steve relayed what had happened at Skull Valley and his hunch that the Thatcher gang could be lying low at the Pomeroy ranch.

It made sense to Ron. Steve saw that his left arm was no longer in a sling. "Mrs. Wardell and Christine aren't up yet," he told Steve. "Ricardo and I took them to a show last night and they'll likely sleep late."

"I've got something to tell them," Steve remembered. "But we won't wake 'em up. It'll keep till I get back from Lynx Creek. Where the devil do you think you're going, boy?"

Ron had taken a saddle carbine down from the wall and was stuffing cartridges into his coat pocket.

214

"To Lynx Creek, Steve, with you and the sheriff."

"You're in no shape for it — with your arm just one day out of a sling."

"It wasn't my gun arm," Ron argued, "and I'm tired of being babied. You say you left Millard behind with Granby. So you'll be outnumbered, five to four, unless I go along."

He couldn't be talked out of it. Except for a stiff left arm he seemed fit enough. "Anyway, I was the one who found that Lynx Creek sign," Ron persisted. "If there's any shooting out there I want to be in on it."

He was stubbornly siding Steve when the two walked into Shull's stable shortly before seven o'clock. Walker, Herbert, and St. John were there, waiting with four saddled horses. "Saddle up another one," Ron insisted.

Again he couldn't be talked out of it. When a posse rode east toward Lynx Creek, five men were in it. Ron Garroway, badgeless, carried only a rifle; the others had both holster and scabbard guns. "What I want to know," Joe Walker puzzled, "is what made Thatcher think Granby had a pot of money out there at Skull Valley. The way he acted he must've been plenty sure of it."

"It doesn't add up," Steve reasoned, "unless someone slipped him a phony tip. Someone who's got it in for Granby."

"That includes just about everybody," Herbert reminded them. "Which is why he needed to hire a bodyguard all these years."

"He picked a sorry one," St. John added grimly, "when he took on Wilkeson. What about whanging down on Wilkie, Sheriff, when we get back to town?"

With a sigh of regret the sheriff shook his head. "Nothing we can charge him with. It's not against the law for a bodyguard to run out on his boss."

They crossed a low, piny ridge and dropped down into Lynx Creek. It was still only a little after eight in the morning when they sighted the Pomeroy buildings. "I may buy this place after all," Ron confided to Steve. "Pomeroy's sister, Ruth Crocker, is in town. Talked to her yesterday. She wants to settle his affairs here, and she made me a rock bottom price."

"What does Chris think of it?" Steve asked guardedly. He wanted to know how close to an understanding Ron and Christine were.

"She thinks," Ron told him, "that I ought to take on John Lee's American ranch in the opposite direction. But Lee wants more dough than I can round up."

Sheriff Walker broke in on them. "I see chimney smoke, boys. Spread out and surround the house. Roy, you slip up to the back door of the barn and count the horses stalled there. If there's five, we'll know it's the Thatcher gang."

Lynx Creek willows were on one side of the house. Steve and Ron were about fifty yards apart as they got into the willows and dismounted. In a meadow about the same distance on the opposite side of the house was a stack of old spoiled hay. Using it for a shield, Joe Walker got behind it. Herbert dismounted, carbine in

216

hand, and made a run for a pile of cordwood about eighty yards from the kitchen door.

Steve looked toward the barn and saw Roy St. John peering over the half-doors there. The deputy was holding up five fingers. It meant that the barn had five horses, which supported the theory that Lou Thatcher and four other outlaws were hiding in the house.

Walker shouted from his haystack, "Come out, Thatcher, with your hands up. It's the law and we've got you surrounded."

The front door opened and Lou Thatcher stood there. He had a rifle in his hand and a holstered forty-five. "You got nothing on me, Sheriff."

"We've got plenty," Walker yelled back. He stepped into full view of Thatcher. "Murder, maybe; depends on whether Granby dies or not."

"Who the hell's Granby?" Thatcher countered. "I don't even know him."

"He knows *you*," the Sheriff barked back. "You raided him and left him for dead. We've got a witness to prove it."

"Yeh? What witness?"

"Fella named Wilkeson. He saw you coming and slipped out the back door."

Thatcher whipped up his rifle and sent a snap-shot bullet toward Walker. The sheriff jumped behind his haystack just in time. In turn, Thatcher dodged back into the house and slammed the door.

Walker shouted, "Let 'em have it, boys."

Steve and Ron fired from the willows. Other rifles cracked from the barn and from the cordwood pile.

217

Every windowpane in the house shattered. The sheriff himself splintered the front door with five fast shots.

A single shot came from a house window. It was aimed at the barn, where the face of Roy St. John had been peering over a half-door.

After that a long silence. A patch of gunsmoke hung over the cordwood pile from which Herbert had fired. Then again Joe Walker made a call for surrender. Again there was an exchange of gunfire between outlaws and lawmen. This time a yell from just inside a window probably meant a hit. It was a window on the creek side, and Steve heard a dismayed voice: "It's Rufe, Thatch; they got him."

It could mean that the odds were now five to four in the law's favor. Steve was fairly sure of it when at the next exchange of gunfire no shot came from Rufe's window.

"We can cut you down one by one," the sheriff shouted.

"Yeh? Come and get us," Thatcher yelled back.

"We don't need to, Thatch. We can just pin you down till you run out of grub and water."

And ammunition, Steve added mentally. But most of all it would depend on the will of the defenders to hold out. Their toughness under fire. Was there a weak one among them?

Suddenly the back door opened and one man came out with his hands raised. He was unarmed, so there was no point in shooting at him. This man had clearly lost his nerve and wanted to surrender.

He never got the chance. A voice in the house yelled, "Jocko's walkin' out on us, Thatch! The rat!"

The desertion must have brought a blinding fury to Lou Thatcher, for immediately he appeared in the kitchen doorway with a rifle stock at his cheek. He fired one bullet, then ducked back inside. It was aimed not at a lawman but at the deserter. The slug hit Jocko between the shoulder blades and dropped him dead in his tracks just before he reached the line of willows.

"Makes us five to three now!" St. John yelled from the barn.

After a few more volleys, voices from the house had a tone of dissension. As though one or more of them wanted to give up; as though one at least was angry at Thatcher for his cold-blooded killing of Jocko.

Again Walker from his haystack and St. John from the barn splintered the front door with bullets. Then the door flew open and three rifles were tossed out. Three belt guns followed. Three men walked out, hands raised. Thatcher was the last of the three and could only raise one hand. His other arm had been struck by a bullet and was useless.

The three stood sullenly in front of the house while Walker and his crew advanced on them with level carbines. "Look in my saddlebags and you'll find some cuffs, Herb."

Deputy Herbert brought two pairs of handcuffs, and they were clamped on the two unhit outlaws. Another man was found dead just inside a front window, and Jocko lay lifeless near the willows. "Makes no difference now whether Granby dies or not," Walker told Thatcher. "We can hang you for your job on Jocko."

St. John looked closely at one of the unhit Hangouters. "I've seen your name on a wanted circular somewhere. Capehart, isn't it? A bank job in Kansas?"

"That was two years ago and I was acquitted," Capehart said. "And it wasn't me who shot Jocko; it was —"

Thatcher, with his good arm, slapped him hard across the mouth.

The other unhit man gave the name of Jones. Steve recalled seeing him at the Hangout bar.

"Herb," Walker decided, "you stick here with the two dead men till the coroner shows up. Rest of us'll hit for the courthouse. Roy, saddle three of their horses."

Presently they were on their way, heading west toward Prescott. Three prisoners and four lawmen. All the way there Walker kept repeating a question. "Who was it tipped you fellas that Granby had a bag of money on him? You sure as hell didn't ride out there for peanuts."

He got no answer out of Thatcher nor from the man who called himself Jones. It was Capehart who gave it away just before they sighted town. "I'd like to get my mitts on that guy!" Capehart blurted out. "Him sayin' Granby had a big stake out there? And all the old geezer had was small change!"

Steve made a shrewd guess. "You mean the lawyer Frank Maxwell?" He remembered that Granby's man Sligo had beat up Maxwell and later had gone after him

220

with a gun, and that Granby had fired Maxwell as the Skyline attorney.

"How did you know?" Capehart spat out bitterly. "Yeh, it was Maxwell, the double-crossin' son-of-a —"

He got no further because Lou Thatcher leaned sideways from his saddle and again his good hand slapped Capehart hard across the mouth.

They rode into the plaza with half the town staring. A jailor met them at a courthouse basement door, and in a very few minutes Thatcher, Jones, and Capehart were in cells there.

Deputy Millard was waiting in Walker's office. "Just got in, Sheriff. Delivered Granby to Mother Monica, and she's got him in a hospital bed."

"What shape's he in?" Steve asked.

"Doctor Day's with him; says he's got less than an even chance. Lost consciousness on the way in. The sisters are fussing over him, doin' what they can."

"Get word to the coroner," Walker ordered, "that he's got two customers out at the Pomeroy ranch." The sheriff stretched wearily. "Right now I'm going to bed and sleep a week."

"What about Frank Maxwell?" Steve asked. "Should we pick him up?"

"Why not? He framed the whole play, didn't he? Passing out that bum tip about Granby. If it hadn't been for Maxwell, Granby wouldn't be dying in a hospital bed and two men wouldn't be dead out on Lynx Creek. Makes Maxwell an accessory, I figure. Go grab him, Roy."

Millard had already left with a message for the coroner. Roy St. John now went on the errand of arresting Maxwell. It should be simple enough; Maxwell, no gunman, would hardly put up a fight. St. John would need only to cross Cortez Street and go up the steps next to the bakeshop. Maxwell should be in either his living quarters or his office.

Ron Garroway, to see the posse's mission to its end, had stuck with Steve all the way to the courthouse. He now left with Steve, angling across the courtyard toward the plaza's bank corner. "I've got something to tell Christine and Mrs. Wardell," Steve remembered. "About what I saw in a ranch guest room —"

He broke off and stood looking at a four-horse stagecoach in front of the Williams House. Passengers were boarding the coach with a small crowd on the walk to see them off. The stage driver leaned idly against the hotel's front, smoking a cigarette.

"You go on to the house, Ron," Steve said, "and wait for me. I'll be along in a few minutes. Want to check on something first."

Ron, mildly puzzled, walked on toward Marina Street. Steve crossed Gurley to the waiting stage. In a few minutes it would be leaving for Banghart, Simms' Camp, Williams, Flagstaff, and End-of-Track. Some of the passengers were already in their seats.

Steve looked into the Williams House lobby and saw others saying goodbye to friends there. He checked with the driver. "You got a passenger list for this trip?"

"Yeh, every seat taken." The driver showed the list, and one of the names on it didn't surprise Steve.

222

All the coach seats except one were now occupied. "That fella better get a move on if he's goin' with me," the driver said. He climbed to his box and took the reins.

"Here he comes now," Steve said.

Frank Maxwell, with a bag in each hand, hurried downstairs to the Williams House lobby. He came out on the sidewalk and was boarding the coach when Steve stopped him.

"You're wanted as an accessory." Steve showed his badge and laid a hand on the lawyer's arm. "The raid on Granby. If he dies it's murder. Sheriff says pick you up."

A whip cracked and a four-horse coach rolled away, heading for a world beyond Yavapai County and leaving Frank Maxwell behind on the plaza walk.

CHAPTER
TWENTY-ONE

The five in Emily Wardell's parlor looked up in breathless suspense at a framed portrait on the wall. Steve Mulgrave had just told them about a faded rectangle on another wall out at the Skull Valley ranch.

"Yes," Emily remembered, "Henry's picture hung there for years — in the guest room. It was one of the few things I brought to town when the place was offered for sale."

"Let us not get too excited," Ricardo Gonzales advised. "After all it is only a possibility."

"I'd call it a probability," Ron Garroway said, "seeing that it's the only place that hasn't been looked in." He was sitting by Christine on the parlor sofa.

Steve got up with a screwdriver in hand. "Shall I operate?" he asked Mrs. Wardell.

At her nod he took the frame down from the wall, turning it over to expose a thin wood backing. A few pries and the backing came off. A sheet of paper fell to the floor.

Steve picked it up, saw that it was filled with writing. "This is it," he said.

The sheet was passed from hand to hand. When Christine saw her father's name, a film of tears clouded her eyes. Gonzales took it from her. "With your permission," he suggested, "I will read it aloud."

He read with a low, solemn eloquence as though he were addressing a courtroom. Steve, Ron, Christine, and Emily listened silently.

> The Wardell Ranch
> Skull Valley
> Sept. 18, 1873

On the way here Isaac Pendleton tried to kill me. I saw his face behind the rifle barrel and am sure Chad Granby told him to do it. Next time they may succeed, so I write this to condemn them in case of my death.

Just after dark on the last Saturday in July Adam Mayberry brought a rich ore sample to me. I knew at once that the claim it came from would be a bonanza. Mayberry wouldn't tell me where the claim was. He had staked it, and would file Monday when the courthouse opened. I promised to have my assay report ready by Tuesday.

Just then Chad Granby walked in. He held a mortgage on all my property and it was overdue. He came to announce immediate foreclosure. I introduced him to Mayberry and pointed out the bonanza silver sample, estimating that it would assay more than a thousand dollars per ton of ore. At once cupidity possessed Granby. He asked Mayberry if he had capital to develop the mine. The answer was no. Many thousands of dollars would need to go in before a penny of profit could come out. Mayberry realized that. Granby offered to furnish the development capital on fair terms — provided he could first see the claim. To this Mayberry agreed. Granby said he wanted to take along a mining expert, a prospector named Pendleton. Again Mayberry agreed. They would ride to the claim early the next day.

This they did, the three of them. But only two of them came back. Granby never told me why. But he made me a proposition and in my weakness I accepted it. He would mark my mortgage paid in full if I would suppress the ore sample Mayberry had brought in and never mention his name.

Soon after that Isaac Pendleton staked a claim on the ridge above Milk Creek and called it the Skyline. He professed to have found it under a fifty-fifty grubstake arrangement with Granby. They became half-and-half owners of it and each made a fortune. I cannot prove that they murdered Mayberry and jumped his claim. But I do know that they left town with Mayberry at dawn that Sunday morning and came back without him, and that Granby met Mayberry at my house that Saturday night. If he denies his guilt, let him explain why, during the long public search for Adam Mayberry, he kept silent.

I shall inform Granby that I have concealed this statement where it will be found after my death. From the family of Adam Mayberry I ask, but do not deserve, forgiveness for my own guilt.

HARLEY ROOD

The mist in Christine's eyes all at once became a flood. She buried her face in her hands and sobbed uncontrollably. For years she'd been resigned to her father's death, but this sudden bald confirmation of it released a long pent-up grief. When Ron impulsively put an arm around her she didn't seem to know it. The others looked on in silent compassion. It made Ron seem closer to her than anyone else, her natural and intimate comforter. Especially to Steve it looked that way.

Gonzales was the first to speak. "May I have your permission, Christine," he asked, "to use this statement as I see fit for the advancement of your interests?"

Mechanically she nodded consent.

"In that case, *con su permiso*," the attorney said, "I shall get busy at once." He put the paper in his pocket, bowed formally to Emily Wardell, and quietly left the house.

Steve, not wanting to sit here any longer and see Ron with his arm around Christine, made his own excuse to Emily. "It's something the law ought to know about, this Rood statement; reckon I better go tell Joe Walker."

He went out and hurried to the courthouse. The sheriff's office was empty. But in a few minutes District Attorney Ferd Oliver came in. He had a paper in hand. "Hello, Steve. Here's something I want served on Wilkeson."

"An arrest warrant?"

Oliver shook his head. "We've got no legal charge against Wilkeson. But we need him as a witness against Thatcher, Jones, and Capehart. Granby himself isn't enough. He's in no shape to be brought into court. And he didn't recognize anyone but Thatcher. This is a subpoena calling Wilkeson as a witness."

Steve understood. The bodyguard had deserted, but not before he'd seen five men riding up to the house. He could be put under oath and asked to identify them. "You want this subpoena served right away?"

"At once," Ferd Oliver said. "The first hearing's set for tomorrow."

It was something to do. Serving a subpoena should be simple enough, so he went out and crossed Montezuma Street to Whiskey Row. He began at Gurley and worked south toward Goodwin. Wilkeson should be in one of the eight saloons in that block.

He inquired at them all, subpoena in hand. "Has Three-Card Wilkeson been in here this morning?" The answer was no at the Nifty, the Capital, the Palace, the Sazerac, Cobweb Hall, the Exchange, Daly's and the Plaza Bit. At Goodwin Steve turned west to cover the several small bars between there and Chinatown.

The Hassayampa Hangout was off Wilkeson's regular beat, but today he bought a whiskey there. It was a good listening post for underworld gossip, and right now he had an especial reason to listen. He knew they'd picked up three of the five Skull Valley raiders and that the other two were dead. His troubling doubt was, Which two were dead?

He hoped that one of them was a man named Jocko. For Jocko could tell a tale on him, a murder tale dating from long ago in Texas. If Jocko had been brought in a living prisoner, he might talk to improve his own

228

position with the law. Everything would be all right if Jocko was one of the two dead men out at the Pomeroy ranch.

This was the bar at which Thatcher and his crew had organized themselves. So there might be talk here about the raid, telling him whether Jocko was alive or dead. For Wilkeson hadn't deserted Granby merely to save his own skin in a one-to-five gunfight. That would have been reason enough — but there'd been another. He'd recognized Jocko as one of the on-coming riders. And even under the best circumstances any confrontation with Jocko was to be avoided.

Was Jocko dead, or was he a prisoner in Joe Walker's jail?

A shabby, shaggy man at the bar nudged Wilkeson. He'd just come in from the street and his husky tip startled the gambler. "They're lookin' for you, Three-Card. Better skin out if you don't want to be picked up."

Wilkeson turned with a jerk. "Who's looking for me?"

"That there special depitty they call Steve. He's got a paper to serve on you and he's asked at every bar on the Row."

A sense of being trapped possessed Wilkeson. It didn't occur to him that the paper could be a mere subpoena. What else could it be but a murder warrant? Jocko, alive and in jail must have talked. That old Texas case was a tight one and meant a noose for him — once a Texas lawman was brought here to identify him.

A sullen fury swept through him, and much of it focused on Steve Mulgrave. For years he'd cheated the law and gotten away with it, ducking charge after charge, including two saloon killings here at Prescott. Now came this cowboy lawman, Mulgrave, to serve a murder warrant with the dust of years on it. Mulgrave, who'd run down Sarg and made a fugitive of Ernie Jacks, and who'd now brought in Jocko with his tale of an old Texas killing!

"You'd better skin out!" the shabby man warned again.

But where could he go? They'd be watching every livery barn and outgoing stage. Where could he go or hide? There was nothing to do but stand here and wait for Mulgrave. He couldn't even shoot it out with Mulgrave, because his holster was empty. To avoid a fine he'd checked his gun at the Palace bar upon arriving from Skull Valley.

A man further down this bar had just ridden in from the range and was still gunslung. His thirty minutes weren't up yet. Wilkeson swallowed the rest of his whiskey and moved along the bar to stand next to the man. His brain seethed with a stubborn resolution. He wasn't going back to Texas to face that murder count. Mulgrave would never take him alive. A time came when a man had to stand and fight. This was the time for Three-Card Wilkeson. "Monte," they'd called him in his Texas days. But only a few, like Ernie Jacks and Buck Sarg and Jocko, knew it.

The half-doors pushed open and Steve Mulgrave came in. He had a badge on his jacket, a gun in his holster — and a paper in his hand. A paper to serve on Wilkeson! He saw Wilkeson at mid-bar. "Been looking all over town for you, Wilkie," he announced.

Wilkeson's hand darted to a holster — not his own but the holster of a man at his elbow. The gun whipped up level with roars and flashes. There was a third roar from the doorway, and Wilkeson's knees buckled under the impact of a breast hit. Only the one shot had come from Steve Mulgrave.

The Hangout customers stood gaping at Wilkeson. He lay face-down on the sawdust floor, a gun still gripped in his hand. It had happened before at the Hangout and would happen again. "What did he do, Deputy?" the bartender asked. "Stick up a stage, maybe?"

"Nothing, far as I know," Steve told them. "We only wanted him as a witness."

The barman leaned over his bar and looked sadly down. "Anyway he's dead. As dead as Rufe and Jocko." But he said it too late to help Wilkeson.

CHAPTER
TWENTY-TWO

Ricardo Gonzales stood in the anteroom of the Sisters of St. Joseph Hospital. This was the third day he'd waited here without being permitted to see Chad Granby.

"He is in no condition," Mother Monica said. Doctor Day had backed her up.

But Gonzales was patient, and this morning he had better luck. Doctor Day came through after making his daily round and saw the attorney there. "All right, Ricardo," he decided. "But make it short. He rallied a little last night. You may have twenty minutes with him, no more."

"What are his chances, Doctor?"

"Nil. His mind is okay, but he had internal injuries which are inoperable. He may hang on a month or so, but I doubt it."

One of the sisters took Gonzales to the hospital's only private ward. Chad Granby lay abed there, looking thin, pallid, old, and broken. The lawyer could count every bone in his face. It was distasteful to present a business matter to him. But his first duty was to his client, Christine Mayberry.

He drew up a chair by the bed. "Please attend what I have to say, Mr. Granby. We have found what you searched for at Skull Valley ranch. See?" He took a paper from his pocket and held it so that Granby could see the signature "Harley Rood."

"I shall read it aloud to you, *Señor*," Gonzales proceeded to read aloud the entire statement found under the backing of a framed portrait.

Granby, weak in body but mentally sound, missed no word of it and understood.

"On the basis of this statement and other evidence," Gonzales informed him, "I shall file suit in behalf of Christine Mayberry for full title to the Skyline mining claim. You will contest that suit — but at the very least we can tie the property up in the courts for years. Whatever title you have will be clouded until the final appeal has been settled. Do you understand?"

After a long stare from hollow eye sockets Granby managed three words: "You cannot win."

"In the end perhaps not. But with injunctions we can tie up every shipment of bullion pending the outcome. You are incorporated, and your stock on the San Francisco mining exchange will drop many points. I do not think that you yourself will be prosecuted for complicity in the murder of Adam Mayberry. We admit that the evidence is old and circumstantial. But three things we do have: the confession of Harley Rood, a bullet in the skull of a horse, and nearby proof that the horse belonged to a man who traveled to Arizona on the steamship *Newbern* in the summer

233

of eighteen-seventy-three. These things will impress a jury, Señor Granby."

Again the faint but stubborn three words: "You cannot win."

"And neither can you, *Señor*. At best it will be a long and costly fight for both sides. So I suggest a compromise. That we settle out of court for one hundred thousand dollars."

Chad Granby looked at him, and Gonzales could sense the wheels of his shrewd business mind churning. This time a clipped two words came from the man's lips: "*Ten thousand*."

Ricardo was prepared for it. "Ninety," he countered.

"Twenty."

"Eighty."

"Twenty," Granby repeated stubbornly. No less stubbornly Gonzales for a while stuck to his figure of eighty thousand.

After minutes of give-and-take they settled for sixty thousand dollars. Gonzales drew from his pocket a contract carefully prepared in advance and with a blank space left for the exact figure of settlement. He wrote in the space the sum agreed upon and called in two of the sisters for witnesses.

Chad Granby, propped up with a pillow at his back, signed, and the instrument was properly witnessed.

"You must go now," one of the sisters insisted, and Ricardo Gonzales, signed contract in hand, was glad enough to be gone.

At the post office Steve Mulgrave picked up a letter from Shorty Brill. "This Lonesome Valley outfit," Shorty wrote, "is a jim-dandy. Good cows, good grass, good grub and plenty of it. Boss says there's a bunk here for you, Steve, if you want it."

It made another prospect, but Steve had better ones. A Date Creek spread had offered him a foremanship. And Joe Walker wanted to keep him on permanently as a Yavapai County deputy. And Steve knew where he could buy the relinquishment on an improved homestead on the lower Hassayampa. He had savings of seven hundred dollars in Sol Lewis's bank, plus a good roan horse and a saddle.

What he really wanted, though, was unattainable. She was already taken, Steve was sure, by Ron Garroway.

An hour later he was surer of it than ever. He'd decided to ride to the lower Hassayampa to look the improved homestead over. He couldn't say good-bye to Emily Wardell because she was away on a short visit to a niece at Phoenix. But he could say good-bye to Christine and Ron.

As he approached the front door of the Marina Street house, he heard voices from the parlor. Christine's and Ron's. They were in there arguing about something. "No, Christine," Ron was saying, "I'd rather take on the Lynx Creek place. Ruth Crocker offers it for nothing down and easy payments. That'll let me use my own stake to buy cows."

"But it can't compare," Christine protested, "with Mr. Lee's American ranch. It's beautiful out there. I've asked Emily and Ricardo and they both agree."

"Lee wants three times as much as I've got," Ron persisted.

"Don't be silly, Ron. I can let you have what you need . . ."

Steve backed away, wanting to hear no more. Only lovers would quarrel like that. And only a girl who'd decided to marry a man would offer to help him buy a ranch.

Circling the house, he went to the backyard cabin and packed a bedroll. He could slip away and write his good-byes from Wickenburg. Next he went to the courthouse to clear everything with Joe Walker. The Wilkeson inquest was over and there were no loose ends to hold him here. "There'll be a deputyship open for you," Walker said heartily, "if you ever want it."

From there he went to the bank to see Sol Lewis. He had to wait half an hour before the bank president finished with a Gilette mine operator who wanted a loan. Then Steve presented his case. "If I buy the relinquishment on an improved homestead, will you stake me to the price of a hundred two-year-old heifers?"

Sol Lewis appraised him with narrowed eyes. "I'd say no to the ordinary cowboy, but to you it's yes — providing there's free government range close by."

Steve gave him the location. "All the open range I need close by. I'm starting right now for a look at it."

"You're the only cowboy I know," Lewis said with a shrewd grin, "who ever saved seven hundred dollars out of his pay. Man like that's bound to wind up on top in the cow business. Best of luck." They shook hands and Steve left the bank.

Then he went upstairs with the idea of saying good-bye to Gonzales. But the lawyer wasn't in, so Steve left a note on his desk. After that he circled the plaza to pay a few small bills and make a purchase or two. At Shull's stable he rented a pack mare. He could load his bedroll and baggage on her and camp out on his way to the lower Hassayampa.

A familiar voice hailed him as he was saddling the roan. "I catch up with you just in time, Estevan." It was Ricardo Gonzales with the breezy briskness of one who brings good news. "There is a man who wishes to see you on a matter of importance."

Steve raised an eyebrow. "Yeh? What's going on, Rick?"

"He is a big cattleman from New Mexico who now controls a fifty-thousand-acre grant in the Mogollons of Arizona. I have known him all my life and he trusts my judgment. Today he asks me to recommend him a man of integrity and experience who will go partners with him. He will stock his land with three thousand cows, and I have given him your name, Estevan. You will look after them on shares. First, of course, he desires an interview. So I have made an appointment for him to meet you at my office."

To Steve the prospect was both attractive and exciting. A share in the calf crop from three thousand cows and was much better than starting a shoestring homestead. "When do I meet him?"

"At one o'clock in my office."

"What's his name, Rick?"

"He is Felipe Ventura from Santa Fe, a man of my own people. His grandfather and mine came from Mexico together, and ran sheep on the Rio Grande."

"At one o'clock in your office? I'll be there, Rick."

It was nearly noon, and Steve went first to a barbershop so that he'd make a clean-cut impression on Felipe Ventura. After lunch at a plaza restaurant he hurried to Gonzales's office, entering it at exactly one o'clock.

The office was empty. Steve sat down to wait.

When he heard footsteps coming up, he supposed it was Ventura. But it was Christine Mayberry who came into the office. She was clearly surprised at finding Steve there. "Hello, Steve. Where's Ricardo?"

He gave her a puzzled look. "Were you expecting to meet him here?"

"Yes. To sign a paper in connection with the Granby settlement."

"He told you to come at one o'clock?"

She nodded. "I'm a minute or two late. Has he been in?"

"No, and I don't believe he's coming, either. Nor a fella named Felipe Ventura. I don't believe there is any Felipe Ventura."

"You were waiting for this Mr. Ventura?"

"That's right. Ricardo headed me off just as I was leaving for the lower Hassayampa."

A hurt look showed on her face. "You mean you were leaving town without even telling me good-bye?"

"I went by the house to see you, Christine. But you and Ron were too busy arguin' about where you wanted to start housekeeping. Ron was voting for Lynx Creek and you —"

She broke in on him. "You mean you thought Ron and I are . . ."

"Aren't you?"

Her cheeks took a rosy flush. "Of course not, Steve. And if you weren't blind you'd know why."

All in a sudden moment of wonder he *did* know why. It was hardly believable, but a tenderness in her eyes told him it was true. With a joyous step he went to her and held her in his arms. He tried to summon words, but the best he could think of were, "Would you live in a cabin on the Hassayampa?"

"Anywhere with you, Stephen."

As he kissed her lips neither of them heard a stealthy step in the hall.

It was Ricardo Gonzales who slipped quietly out of an adjacent office. Ricardo put an ear to the door of his own office a moment. A significant silence came from within, and he was satisfied.

He went down to the sidewalk and crossed diagonally to the Williams House. In the bar there he found three of his cronies. This was a small, orderly bar quite unlike the garish ones along Whiskey Row. Mainly it was patronized by courthouse people and the plaza merchants.

The three at the bar were Judge Carttier, Sol Lewis, and Colin Bashford. "This round is on me," Gonzales insisted.

Fred Williams himself filled the glasses. "Once," said Judge Carttier, "I saw a cat who had just stolen the cream. But his grin was not half so smug as yours, Ricardo. Is it because of the settlement you made in the Mayberry case? Hope you got a nice fee out of it."

"A substantial one" Ricardo assured them. "But only in this last hour did I really earn it." He raised his glass. "To my friends Christina and Estevan, *Señores*. May their children be many — in our land of Yavapai."